ONE GIRL FIVE HUNGRY BEASTS

HUTCHINS HUTCHINS

INTRODUCTION

Pick five.
Pick them yourself, or we'll pick them for you.

But... but how will I know who's my baby daddy!?

It's my twenty-eighth birthday.

They have imprisoned me to stop me from escaping.

They know I don't want to be taken by the wolves - I'd rather be dead.

But still, I'm taken, sold off by my own family for a few of coins.

Let's keep it real; my parents never loved me.

I'm half expecting the wolves to eat me or something.

But instead, I'm taken to a ceremonial palace.

I am to pick five husbands...
I will live with them in a marriage home.

Yeah, you heard that right.

I'll also be expected to bear their children.
The more children, the better...

Like, seriously!?

I had barely accepted the idea of just one normal husband.
But five werewolf shifter husbands!?
They can turn into vicious animals at the slightest provocation...
Five hungry, aggressive men who have not seen a woman in 100 years...

Yeah, *100* years.

How could I possibly handle all *that*?

CHAPTER 1

I peer through the leaves at the villagers below, rushing about as they organise my end-of-life party. Not that they would call it that, of course. This is a celebration – I'll be twenty tomorrow, an adult, free to marry, move out of my parent's home and be free from their interference.

At least, that *would* have been my future if I wasn't the first-born daughter, *or* if we didn't live in a place where the first-born daughter of every family is sacrificed to the Werewolves that have overtaken our world. Or maybe they'd fight to let me stay if we'd had a string of first-born daughters to sacrifice. Unfortunately, I was the first female born to our village in a decade. While the villagers around us thrived from the wealth given them for every woman sacrificed, our village was desperately poor, and desperately in need of the tributes the werewolves paid in return for every human female.

Not that you can see that today. There's a pig cooking over one spit and a row of chickens over another. Our chief, Vallin, leads a line of young men, each carrying a keg of his famous mead, toward the stage where the musicians, a harpist and a fiddler are already tuning up. The scent of roasted potatoes and parsnip fill the air, mingling with my mother's apple pie and something that smells like hot raspberries.

It's making my mouth water, but that's at odds with the churning in my stomach, the awareness that today is my last day here, and everyone is celebrating. No one cares that they'll never see me again.

"Martha? What are you doing up there?" I glance down to see Odran's green eyes peering up through the leaves of the oak tree at me. He's long and lanky, and he swings up through the branches like a monkey, so nimble he looks like he was born in the tree, rather than under it.

He perches himself on the branch beside me, gazing out through the gap to see where I'm looking.

"Ah." He nods. "Celebration preparation." He glances at me, his mouth turned down. "Except not so celebratory for some of us." Odran is my oldest friend. My only friend, really. People seem to shy away from forming friendships with someone who is only going to be sacrificed one day. Even the younger girls, first-born daughters in their own families, keep to themselves. It's like we're all too scared to admit what the future holds, and seeing each other is just a reminder of what's to come.

"Some of us?" I snort. "I think the only people not looking forward to this party are you and me. I don't even understand why they insist on going through with this."

Odran starts cleaning the dirt out from under his fingernails. "Well, you know—" He glances for a moment out at the bustle below us. "They do want to make this special for you. It's not like any of them *made* the law. They just have to follow it. They're using up the best of everything to make your last night with us something special."

"Ha! They're using the best of what we've got because they know that tomorrow they'll have new and better everything! You've heard Nesta's stories – in her home village the previous first-born tribute included a new plough! But that's not the only reason—" My lower lip begins to tremble and I stop, clenching my jaw until the sensation goes away.

"They're celebrating getting rid of me. Halleluiah – cranky Martha is going to be werewolf supper, and we'll never have to put up with her again."

Odran put an arm around me. "You know that's not true."

"Do I?" I glance at him, and he pulls his arm back. "I don't fit in here, I never have. But I sure as hell don't deserve to be sent off to a pack of werewolves." I look at him. "Why do you suppose they take us?"

Odran cringes. "Maybe we should talk about something else."

I frown. "Why? Shouldn't I contemplate my last moments?"

"I think you should spend your last moments on happy thoughts, instead of sad ones."

"Do you think I'll be tastier? If I'm happier I mean. Less stressed and all that. Father always said that if you kill an animal quickly they always taste better than when you do a whole herd at once. The ones in the pen always seem to know what's coming, and they make such a pitiful noise, and then the meat tastes terrible. Perhaps the werewolves deserve to have terrible tasting meat."

"You don't know that, Martha." Odran is frowning, his eyes troubled. "No one knows for sure what happens."

"No. No one does. But everyone *believes* we're food for them, and it's just as likely that as anything else."

"So maybe you should run away." Odran's voice is so soft, I'm not sure I've heard right.

"Run away?" I've never thought about such a thing, but now Odran has suggested it, my thoughts begin to race.

He shrugs. "Sure, why not. It's not that far to the next village."

I shake my head. "I couldn't run to Nesta's village, they'd send me back. If word got out that I'd run, no village would be safe. But the city—" I turn to Odran, my eyes wide. "If we could get as far as Ivlocaster I could hide amongst all the people there. They'd never find me."

Odran's Adam's apple bobs as he swallows. "The city is huge, and so far away." He must see the expression on my face because he stops and takes a deep breath. "The city. Okay, we can try for the city."

"We?" I frown.

"I couldn't let you go alone. I'd have to come with you."

"Oh, Odran!" I wrap my arms around him. "That is the sweetest thing anyone has ever said to me. But you can't leave." I pull away, holding him at arm's length. "What about Dasha? You two are promised to marry as soon as she becomes of age. You can't break that promise."

Odran shrugs and looks away. "There are plenty of men to take my place."

"No." I shake my head. "Dasha chose you. She loves you. You love her! Don't you dare force her to have someone she doesn't want. It's bad enough *I* have to go through with this." My gaze returns to the movement in the village square. "I wouldn't wish this on anyone."

"I had a feeling you might say that." Odran sighs and hands me a bag. "There's enough supplies in here to last two people two days. If you can ration it you should get a week, longer if you supplement it with a bit of foraging and fishing. I don't know how far it is to the city or what is available between here and there. If I'd thought you'd want to go to the city itself, I would've snuck you more supplies."

My eyes begin to prickle, and I blink away tears. "Oh, Odran. You've read my mind! That is so sweet! Dasha really is a lucky girl to have you."

"Yeah." Odran slides off our perch to stand on the branch below. "Stay safe, Martha. Look after yourself, all right."

I hug the bag to my chest as I watch Odran swing down through the trees. I'll miss Odran. I might even miss Dasha, though I'm sure I only feel protective of her because she's my younger sister. There seems to be some sort of rule about families, that they have to look out for each other, even if they can't stand one another. At least, that's how my parents seem to see the world. I annoy them at every moment. I don't even need to try. They never say as much, but I can tell. I don't get hugs like the rest of my siblings, or special acknowledgement, or any indication that they're aware of my existence. Except when there is potential danger, and then they're super protective of me, constantly warning me about the risks of everything from riding a bike to climbing a tree.

Not that I ever listened to them. I've known from the moment I could talk that I was going to be a sacrifice one day. There's no way known I was going to miss out on *any* life experience, not when my life was going to be cut short, and I was going to miss out on the most important ones.

. . .

I STAY in the tree for the rest of the afternoon. There doesn't seem to be much point in joining in the hustle and bustle, and if I climb down before sunset, someone is sure to see me and my newly acquired bag.

I'm not supposed to have any worldly goods. Clothes are exempt, of course, but other than that I have nothing of my own, just shared items, belonging to my family, or me and my siblings. No point personalising something for someone who is just going to die. If someone sees me with the bag, they'll have a whole lot of questions that I really don't feel like answering.

I wonder how Odran will explain its absence. And will they automatically assume he was the culprit when they find me and the bag, not to mention the several days' worth of food, missing?

The sun sinks to the west and finally the bonfire is lit, and the musicians start to play. I can't believe no one has come looking for me yet. Am I really that unimportant that they don't even need me for my starring role?

That would show them, wouldn't it? The werewolves come for their sacrifice, and she's not even here. I wonder if that's ever happened before. I wonder what the werewolves would do. Do they take another young girl? I feel a twinge of guilt at that. Dasha is the next oldest, just twelve months younger than me. My parents must've been thrilled, blessed with two daughters in such a short space of time.

One to sacrifice for the good of the village, one to marry off for the good of themselves.

But that was being cynical. They obviously loved Dasha. They hugged her whenever she cried, whereas I got sent from the room for making everyone miserable. Come to think of it, they hugged her if she ever had anything to celebrate, as well. I never had anything to celebrate. There was no point in doing well at the village school, or learning how to embroider in neat fine stitches, or to weave strong baskets, if I was just going to be food for the werewolves. I'm certain if Dasha had been the oldest, they would've fought to save her.

I shake my head. Everyone tells me I'm being foolish. Of course my parents love me. I'm just different than Dasha, like chalk and cheese as the saying goes. It makes sense they'd love me differently.

I just wish I could see signs of it myself.

Dasha and I had been so close, once. It's not her fault we're not now. I just got so jealous off all the things that she had, and I stopped talking to her, even though she tried to share what she could. She hated our parents for treating us so differently. Why did I turn against her and not them? I sigh. There's little point dwelling on a past I can't fix. It's too late now.

I turn my mind back to wondering about the werewolves. Perhaps if there is no sacrifice they'll simply tear the village to shreds. I smile at that thought. That would serve the villagers right, for being so horrid. But then Odran and Dasha's faces flash through my mind and that twinge of guilt turns into a stab.

Even if the rest of the village were flesh-eating cannibals, I can't let the village be destroyed with Odran and Dasha in it.

I can't let either of them be hurt.

I thrust Odran's bag into a hollow in the tree. I'll let him know where it is. Hopefully he'll be able to get back to it before the food goes bad.

Finally, I descend, scrubbing at my tears with the side of my hand. I don't want them to see I've been crying. I'm not tall like Odran, so there's a little more scrambling to lower myself from branch to branch.

The bottom branch is a little way off the ground, and I have to wrap my arms around it and swing down, dropping to land on the soft grass beneath.

I land with a thud, and a millisecond later there's a hand on my shoulder.

"Going somewhere, Martha?"

I spin around to see my father, his lips set in a thin line.

"Just coming to see you, actually."

"I'm sure." He wraps one arm around my shoulders and directs me away from the village green.

"Where are we going?"

"The villagers don't actually need to see you, tonight. Everyone thinks you've been chatting with everyone else, and they're okay with that. They can rest easy in the knowledge that we've thrown you a fine party. Seeing you will just make them feel bad. We've got a delicious meal for you in Vallin's rooms, everything you love. You can stay there tonight, and then tomorrow he'll take you out to the ceremonial platform. You don't need to worry your pretty little self about anything except making it to the platform in one piece."

I try to pull away, but father's grip is tight. "You've even got some mead, a whole jug of it all to yourself. You're welcome to drink yourself into oblivion, if that helps."

"Where's mother and Dasha?"

Father shrugs. "Your disappearance this afternoon has caused both of them some heartache. Your mother sent me to find you. She was terrified we'd have to send Dasha off to the werewolves, and that set your sister into hysterics. Your mother has had to stay with her, to comfort her." He shakes his head. "You never think of anyone else, do you? All this heartache and stress could've been avoided if you'd just stayed in your room like you were supposed to."

We reach Vallin's rooms, where one of Vallin's heavily built guards is waiting.

"Keep an eye on her, will you? Make sure she doesn't harm herself. She needs to be pristine for the exchange tomorrow."

Pristine? I nearly snort with laughter. As if I am pristine. More like the ugly duckling from that old fairy tale, except that in this case I never grew up to be the swan.

Father turns to me. "You behave yourself, for once in your life. This is the most important thing you will have ever done. Don't ruin it for the rest of us."

Vallin's guard takes my arm and pulls me through the main room, into one of Vallin's guest rooms. There's a bed in one corner and a table laden with food: roast pork and chicken, all sorts of roast vegetables, fresh fruit, apples and plums and raspberries and blueberries and grapes. There's fresh bread, and cheese and butter and jam, and to one side my mother's apple pie, with hot raspberry sauce.

And the mead. A whole jug of it, just for me. Perhaps I could drink the lot of it. I'd known adults to wake with no memory of their actions on the previous day. Maybe not knowing what was happening to me would be best.

The smell is to die for, and I quickly realise that is probably exactly what is about to happen to me. No one has actually witnessed what happens at a werewolf sacrifice, but the women are never seen again, so there doesn't seem to be any other explanation for what happens. Still the thought isn't enough to stop my mouth from watering. I take a grape, savouring the burst of flavour on my tongue as my teeth break the skin.

"May as well eat up." Vallin's guard takes a chair by the window, leaning back in it so the front legs lift of the floor. "Got a big day tomorrow. Who knows when you'll eat again."

I'll get to eat again? What a curious thing to say. Why would the werewolves feed someone they were going to eat? Unless I wouldn't be eaten straight away.

I survey the food before me. Maybe I'll be able to run away *after* I've been taken by the werewolves. Then they wouldn't have to take the next oldest girl *or* destroy the village. Odran and Dasha would be safe, and I could be free.

Werewolves are known to be fast, though, and strong. I'll need to keep my wits about me. And for that I'll need food.

My stomach growls. I turn away from the mead and instead take a hunk of roast pork.

I'm going to make the most of this meal. Because even if it's not my last meal ever, it might be the last feast I have for a very long time.

CHAPTER 2

I wake up feeling ill. The night before I gorged myself, devouring all the meat and vegetables, my mother's entire apple pie and a good portion of the bread and cheese.

I probably would've finished off the bread and cheese, except a tiny voice in my head suggested these were things I could hide in my pockets, something to snack on if I needed to keep my strength up.

Now I wished I'd come to that realisation before I'd started eating, and had downed some of the fruit instead.

The last thing I feel like doing is eating more, but Vallin wakes me up, suggesting I eat some breakfast before we continue on our way. I didn't want to make him suspicious so I ate some of the berries, sliding an apple in the pocket not holding the bread and cheese. It looks a bit bulky, but I was hopeful no one would notice.

"Do I get to say goodbye to anyone?"

Vallin looks annoyed at this, and I wonder whether he has ever done this before. Surely the last sacrifice must've been before he became chief.

"I'm about to be sent off to feed a pack of werewolves. Surely I get to say goodbye?"

"You said your goodbye's to Odran yesterday, up the tree." He gives me a pointed look, and I wonder whether he was aware of my location before Odran found me. "No one else wants to say goodbye to you."

"What about what I want?"

"You've always been selfish, haven't you? You have no idea how hard this is for our village, sending off one of our young women to the wolves. Do you want to make it harder? People don't need to be reminded of what it is that's about to happen to you. It's far too distressing for all of us. Much better if you behave like the strong martyr you're supposed to be and let it go. It will help all of us move on a lot sooner."

I open my mouth to respond, but I can't think of a single retort that would be biting enough to hurt him, or even give me some satisfaction against his horrid words.

He nods at his guard, who grabs my arm and pushes me out the door. We don't even pass through the village, skirting instead around to the back of Vallin's hut and following a newly made path through the trees to a clearing, several hundred yards away.

I wonder if I scream will anyone be able to hear me And if they can, whether they will even care.

The guard ties my wrists together behind my back, and then attaches the other end of the rope to a tall pole that's been hammered into the ground. He steps back, standing by Vallin's side just within the shelter of the trees.

"What happens now?" I call, as loud as I can, in the hope someone will hear me and feel bad for what they're doing.

Vallin shakes his head. "We wait."

"You're going to watch?" My heart is racing, and I'm fighting not to cry.

"We have to make sure you don't escape," Vallin says with a nod and bile rises in the back of my throat. These werewolves might eat me, but Vallin and his guard are the real monsters. I cannot imagine how anyone could watch someone else be devoured, right before their eyes.

I decide then that I'm not going to be the strong martyr Vallin wants me to be. I'm going to scream as soon as the werewolves appear. I'm going to let it all out, all the fear and anger and sorrow that's been building up all these years, as loud and as shrill as I possibly can.

Let them all feel guilty for what they're doing to me.

As soon as I have the thought there's a rustling in the bushes, on the opposite side of the clearing to where Vallin and his guard stand. I turn my head, opening my mouth in preparation to scream, but before I even lay eyes on the creatures my bounds are cut and I'm thrown over the shoulder of one of them, winded, my scream turning into a gasp as all the breath is knocked out of me. Next thing I know I'm being bounced through the woods.

I get a brief glimpse of the overly large crate they've left behind, Vallin and the guard racing to it, in the moments before the trees close around us. I twist my head, desperate to see who has me, and who else is near. I can see another of the creatures out of the corner of my eye, and I'm sure I hear the sound of three lots of paws, pounding the earth beneath us, but I can't make out anything that might help me get myself out of this situation. All the bouncing is jolting my stomach and making me sick.

I can feel the apple pressing into my stomach, and it's all I can do not to vomit all over the werewolf that's carrying me. I don't want to make them mad, not if they're going to keep me alive for a bit longer. I don't want to give them a reason to kill me early, or take me back to my tribe, like some sort of defective product.

. . .

I DON'T KNOW how long we travel. I'm bounced and bumped around, with little concern for my well-being at all, for what feels like hours. I'm scratched by passing branches, and I'm fairly certain I must have bruises on both my legs from where the werewolf is gripping me.

So much for Vallin's insistence I be kept in 'pristine' condition. The werewolves clearly don't give a damn about that.

I catch glimpses of the other two werewolves out of the corner of my eye. They run on two legs, like a human, though their back legs and tail certainly look dog-like. One has grey fur, the other is more brown, while the one who is carrying me has fur that is pitch black, darker than any I've ever seen on any other creature.

When we stop, the sun is barely any higher than it was when they collected me, making a lie of the time that seemed to pass while I was carried around. I'm surrounded by landscape I've never seen before in my life.

The trees are familiar, but they're so sparse here, and the grass is long and more golden than green. Pretty little flowers dot the plain, white and purple and blue. The land stretches for miles. Behind us is the forest, a mountain looming above it, the very same mountain my village must be on the other side of. There are more mountains in front of us, across the other side of the plain, soft grey and purple and blue lumps on the far horizon, gentle hills undulating between here and there.

The werewolves pause to catch their breath and take a drink from the stream nearby. When they're on all fours they look just like enormous dogs, but when they stand up it's easier to see there is something human about them. Their paws seem very hand-like, with long finger-like pads. The skin is still thicker and rougher, and sharp claws emerge from the ends of each finger. The hair on their chests and stomachs is thin enough to reveal well-toned muscles. One is clearly female, despite her breasts being small and covered with a thin layer of brown fur.

"The city is that way." It's the first time I hear the werewolves speak, and I realise that the one who carried me is talking to me, his arm stretched out to the south. "That's where we're headed. We'll have a break to eat, and then continue on our way. We should be there by late this evening."

It's so strange, to have human words emerge from the snout of a wolf, even one who is standing on his hind legs. His voice is deep and gruff, but his pale blue eyes, almost lost in that mess of pitch-black fur, are kind, and when he undoes the rope chaffing against my wrists, I thank him.

"There's nothing to be afraid of here," he says. "Despite what you may have heard." He taps his chest. "I'm Wulfrun, and this is Kirela, and Guthram." Wulfrun gestures at the other two werewolves, who each nod as their name is spoken. Kirela is the brown one, and Guthram the grey coloured one.

They watch me for a moment in silence, and then Kirela speaks. "What is your name?" Her voice is soft, and if I hadn't picked up that she was female earlier, it would have been unmistakable now.

"Me?" I didn't expect they would actually want to know my name. "Oh, sorry. I'm Martha."

"Martha." Guthram speaks. "It is a pleasure to meet you. A shame it isn't under better circumstances."

My mind is whirling. "So… you're not going to eat me?"

Kirela gives a short sharp bark that I guess is supposed to be a laugh. "Eat you? No. Why on earth would you think that?"

I shrug, my face burning. "That's what they say. No first-born daughter is ever seen again, so people say that they're eaten." I glance at Kirela. "They say that werewolves are strong because you eat the flesh of virgins."

Kirela laughs again. "You humans have strange ideas." She shakes her head. "Werewolves are strong because of our genetic makeup – not because of what we eat. Though I guess it's true of any race, that those who eat healthy meals are stronger than those who don't."

"But why take me like that then? Why the grab and run?"

Wulfrun speaks up. "We've been attacked, in the

past. Some villagers don't want to part with their first-born daughters, and when we've arrived to collect them we've been ambushed. If we're in wolf form we can move faster than any human can react. Better for us to grab you and get out of there. No fighting then. We save a lot of lives that way."

So, other first-born daughters *are* fought for. I try to ignore the stab in my chest and focus on learning as much as I can.

"So… why did you take me? What happens now?"

Wulfrun speaks again. "There is a shortage of females amongst our species. And it was discovered some time ago that we can actually interbreed with humans, so—"

"You're going to breed with me?" I take a step back and shake my head. No way am I going to let that happen!

"It's unlikely to be me personally, unless you pick me. But yes, other men. And only if you agree to it. Rape is abhorrent to us. You will never be forced into something you don't like." Wulfrun raises his front paws in what I'm assuming he hopes is a placating gesture, but his long claws and sharp, pointed teeth just emphasis how powerless I am in this situation and I can feel my heart racing in my chest.

I look Wulfrun up and down. He's hairier than a dog, and vaguely humanoid as he is, his arms and legs look much more wolf like than human. I don't even really want to think about it, but his bits are short and stumpy, mostly hidden in a fold of skin.

There's no way I'll ever have sex with one of these creatures. The very thought of one of them touching me makes me feel ill. I've got to get away from them. And yet I've just experienced how fast they move. I can't rely on speed. Any escape will have to be by stealth.

Kirela is watching me. "We're all werewolves, Martha. You know what that means, don't you?"

I frown. "Of course, I know what it means."

"So, you realise that our current form is not our everyday appearance?"

It takes me a moment to realise that she means that they're actually human-looking, most of the time, and the relief I feel when I realise I don't actually have to have sex with someone looking as they do is immense.

"Oh. Right. Of course. Sorry."

Kirela waves a hand. "Never mind. You've been through a lot today, with plenty of stress leading up to it, by the sounds of things. And your day is not over yet." She glances up at the sky. "We don't have much more time before we need to continue on our way. We should take a moment to refresh ourselves and have a bite to eat before we must go."

Guthram pulls a pack from somewhere, and they share a flask of fresh cool water and some food. I accept the food they pass me, eating the dried fruit and sliding the piece of meat jerky into my pocket when I'm certain they aren't watching. I don't know whether they are telling the truth or not, and if I need to escape quickly, having some food on hand will make it much easier.

Too soon it's time to go, but instead of throwing me over his shoulder, this time Wulfrun kneels so I can climb onto his back, my arms wrapped around his neck, my legs around his body.

"Hold on," he says, before glancing at the others. "Ready?"

They nod, and with a whistle Wulfrun is off, Guthram and Kirela keeping stride with him as we race across the plains.

It seems to me that we are going faster here, no branches or tree roots to dodge or jump over, and yet in other ways it feels as though we are going slower. It's so much easier to see everything, now I'm not being carried like a sack of potatoes. The distant mountains stay distant for such a long time, only the few trees scattered across the landscape giving me any indication of our progress.

Before too long my arms and legs are aching from holding on for so long, but Wulfrun never even calls back to ask me how I'm doing, let alone stops to give me a break. In fact none of the three seem out of breath at all. Are they just fit? Or is super-human speed and endurance simply one aspect of being a werewolf?

Still, I wish they could go faster, or that they'd knocked me out before we went any further. It's giving me far too much time to think back to my family, my village, and especially Odran. What are they doing now? Celebrating their prizes, I guess. From the size of those crates there must've been something decent in there, maybe a new hand plough, certainly plenty of food and seed for the coming year, and probably plenty of things we can't grow ourselves, though I struggle to imagine what. When Nesta's sister was taken, so she told us, their payment included a device that was powered by the sun, that people could watch stories play out on the screen, but that sounds so far out we all thought she was making that one up.

I wonder, does anyone miss me, aside from Odran?

I remember the day he joked he was going to ask my father if he could marry me. Of course I dismissed it, everyone knew I was never going to marry one of the village boys. And I had laughed, too, because if some miracle had freed me from becoming a sacrifice, I'd decided I would never marry. I'd never be tied down to someone, always dependent on their whim, no matter how nice they were.

Still, when my father announced, only days later, that Odran and Dasha were to marry, I couldn't quite squash the disappointment. Dasha had gazed at him so lovingly, and he had avoided me all evening, he wouldn't even make eye contact.

I shake my head. There's no point thinking about any of that now. It didn't matter that I *might've* broken my no-marriage rule for Odran, that time had passed, and I'd been sacrificed, and here I was. Better to let the past lie.

We come to the crest of a hill, and finally the werewolves stop. But Wulfrun doesn't put me down.

"There's the city," Kirela says, pointing down the valley to the huge spires rising up in the distance. "We're almost there."

CHAPTER 3

The city is vast. I know its size is nothing compared to the plains we just crossed, but even so it seems to be hours between the time we first enter the outermost rim of suburbia, and the time we come to the tall, tall buildings in the city centre.

Our pace is slowed in the city. No more running, though the werewolves' walking pace is still so much faster than anything I could ever manage. The city is a bustle of people, and they *are* people. No werewolves to see here, every person could be human, though I strongly suspect that's not the case.

Most people are too busy to pay us any attention, until a small boy lets out a cry and points, and then everyone seems to be looking my way, cheering Wulfrun and the others on.

Are the werewolves I'm with famous? It can't be me everyone is excited to see.

It takes me too long to realise that there are not many women here in the city, and I squirm in Wulfrun's arms. Wulfrun has spoken about the low numbers of female werewolves. Is that why everyone is staring? Are they excited to see a female, or any species?

We stop outside a huge building, and I'm finally able to slide off Wulfrun's back. My legs are so sore I take a moment to stretch them out, rubbing at my sore calves and thighs, shaking my arms to get the blood flow back to my fingers. It takes me a moment to see how grand the building is that we have stopped in front of, but when I do I literally gape in awe.

The building is quite small, in comparison to the neighbouring buildings that seem to scrape the sky, and yet it would still easily cover my entire village back home. The roof is arched, and like the grand columns rising above the marble staircase, completely covered in gold. Behind the columns, heavy red curtains form the walls, the narrowest gap creating a doorway through which I can see light and people.

It's so incredibly different from my own village, in every possible way, that I'm having trouble processing it.

"Come on." Kirela leads the way up the stone steps, Wulfrun and Guthram following behind.

Inside there's a rush of noise, so loud I'm certain they must have a waterfall somewhere in the palace walls. Kirela leads me down a side corridor, leaving Wulfrun and Guthram behind, and into a large room where several other female werewolves and human women wait.

"Are we all here?"

I glance around to see an older woman, grey curls covering her head, and extending, barely visible, down either side of her face.

Is she a werewolf, too?

I've no time to ask any questions before myself and the other women are led out a different door in to a massive room. There is a thunderous applause, and I realise it's the chatter of all these people that I mistook for a waterfall earlier.

I take a step back, and bump into the woman behind me.

"Come on." Kirela offers me a smile as she takes my elbow. "It'll be all right. You'll see."

I swallow my nerves and allow Kirela to lead me out and onto a narrow walkway, several feet above the level where everyone else is standing.

I glance out at the roaring crowd, my chest tightening as I realise there are even less women in this room than there were outside in the city.

What is this? Some sort of slave auction?

At the end of the walkway is another stage, this one lined with men three or four deep.

The women are spread out single file, and Kirela

tells me to have a look at the men and let her know if any appeal.

"What?"

"This is where you pick your possible future partners," Kirela explains. "You need to select five men, and if things work out well, you may end up having sex with one or all of them."

"All of them? Five men? What the actual—"

My words are drowned out as the crowd roars it's approval. One of the women further down the line has picked her five men and is walking off the stage with them.

"How on earth am I supposed to select five men, based on appearance alone, to potentially sleep with? And five of them! Why can't I just pick one?"

Kirela gives me another smile. "I mentioned before that we don't have many women in our population. Because of this, we practise polyandry. It gives more men the chance to have their needs fulfilled and increases the chances of fertility, in case one or more of the men is infertile."

"But, five men! How can you expect any woman to manage five men? How can you possibly allow it?"

Kirela's eyes narrow, and I sense for the first time that I've crossed a line.

"Our race was dying out." She speaks slowly, enunciating every word to make sure I hear and understand. "We came to your planet in the hopes we could take some of your women, not all, just a few, to help build our female population up again. But instead of giving us that option, your King declared war, and not just on us. He killed most of the human female population as well."

I frown. That's not what I was taught. I always thought the werewolves had invaded and killed all our women. There was a war, but didn't it end with a treaty? Isn't that why the first-born daughter is sacrificed? So that the werewolves' desire for blood is sated and the rest of the females can go free?

"If your King had allowed us free passage onto your planet, we might've been able to mingle with you humans, to see who we could attract, who might willingly come. But he didn't, and so instead we had to take over, not only to save our own race, but to save yours as well."

This bit doesn't match what I know. "You took over to take us, not to save us. Why else would you take the first-born daughter of every family, when our own population is so small."

Another cheer rent the air as another woman selected her men and left the stage with them.

Kirela sighs. "We tried to use technology to improve our population. We harvested eggs and sperm from werewolf and human alike, we created babies in the lab, and impregnated any woman who would willingly carry a hybrid baby. But that is no good for the men in our population. Reports of rape and physical violence soared. Male werewolves were fighting to the death. We had to find a way to fix the problem."

I eye off the men opposite me, eyes wide with excitement, watching the next woman in line to see if she'd pick them. I shuddered at the thought of having to touch any one of them.

But then I think back to my own village. So many men left to find wives elsewhere. Some never returned, and we'd hear on the grapevine that they'd died in a fight for a woman, or they'd been executed because they committed some terrible crime, either against a woman or her husband.

"So, this polyandry works then?"

Kirela shrugs. "Nothing is perfect. But if you look at the statistics, then yes, it works. Rapes are down to one or two a year. Physical fights still happen, but only between the men. It seems that the possibility of attracting a woman enough that she will have intercourse with you gives the men enough to focus on." She turned her gaze to the men opposite, but now she turns back to me. "And they do focus on that, Martha. Your husbands will do their absolute utmost to woo you. This lifestyle may sound terrible, but every woman I have ever spoken to says she has never felt more wanted, *more loved*, in her life."

I gaze out over the men again. They are all very human looking, but not one of them is attractive to me from this side of the room.

"What if I can't pick five men. What if I don't want to?"

Kirela nods. "That's perfectly fine. In that case, five will be randomly assigned to you."

I cringe, but really what other choice do I have? Even if I pick the men myself it will still be a random selection. It's not like I know any of them.

"Fine. Good. Pick them. I have no preferences."

Kirela raises an eyebrow, but nods, and when it's my turn she selects the five standing closest to me. I feel cheated, for some reason, like she didn't even bother to pick out the five best options. Then again, maybe she doesn't know them all. In a city this big it would be impossible to know everyone. Perhaps I'm being too hard on her.

They grin, and though they are human, there is definitely something wolfish about the expression, something hungry and predatory.

I shiver, but Kirela pushes me forward and I'm suddenly in the midst of these tall, muscular men. We head into another room where Kirela suggests the men introduce themselves.

The first one steps forward. He has dark shaggy hair and brown eyes. His chin is held high, and he acknowledges me with a slight inclination of his head.

"I am Thyrius," he says, holding out a hand.

I realise just how much my hands are sweating and wipe them on my shirt before I reach out to shake his.

The next one is slouched, his hair much longer than any of the others, reaching past his shoulders, his eyes grey. "Merric," he says with a nod, his hands wedged into the pockets of his trousers.

"Merric," I repeat, and return the nod.

The next one steps forward, his hand held out to take mine. "Ronther," he says, his handshake enthusiastic, to say the least.

I'm already convinced that there are too many men to remember each of their names when the fourth fellow steps forward. "My name is Tormod." His words are pronounced, likes he's speaking a second language and when he shakes my hand, which already feels like it's been held up for far too long, he raises his brow and flashes me a wide grin. He seems friendly at least.

The last man steps forward, pushing strands of black hair out of his deep blue eyes. He's much more attractive than the others, though it's not enough to make me want to have to breed with him. He's staring so intently into mine that I have to glance away.

"You don't recognise me?"

I raise an eyebrow. "Should I?"

He holds out a hand, and when I take it he covers mine with his other.

"I'm Wulfrun." He holds my gaze, as realisation crosses my face.

"You brought me here today."

He nods, a grin crossing his face. "I did. I hope you can forgive me. Neither of us really have a say in our destinies."

I frown, but then Kirela is talking to me again and I have to push his words aside so I can concentrate.

"—you'll be attending University for the first few years here. It's of utmost importance that you learn as much as you can about our shared history and the society we are trying to build here today. You will also need to learn enough to be involved in stimulating and intelligent conversations. Your current knowledge and understanding of the world will have you feeling very much left out and that will not make for a smooth transition into your new life. We do like to make it as easy as possible."

I open my mouth, I want to tell her what an insult it is that she assumes I have nothing interesting or intelligent to talk about, but then I realise that two of the men are talking to each other, and I can't understand a single word they say.

"Merric and Ronther are from Lonrestea," Wulfrun explains. "They speak a different language than the rest of us. Well, except for Tormod, who also speaks another language. He is from Chestranor."

Tormod nods, and begins to speak to me in his own language.

I shake my head. "Can't you just speak English?"

Tormod shakes his head.

I turn to Kirela. "How am I supposed to form a relationship with someone, three someones, who I can't even communicate with?"

It's beyond ridiculous, though I don't say that bit

out loud. I'm still not convinced that they're not going to just eat me later. Perhaps this is like what I said to Odran, about stressed animals not being as tasty. Perhaps they're just trying to calm me down so I taste better when the time comes to eat me.

CHAPTER 4

Kirela smiles and holds up two tiny slivers of what looks like metal.

"You are about to have these implanted into your neck," she said. "One is a translator chip, so that any language you hear is translated into your own language, and the other is a hard drive chip. It allows you to store necessary information that you access through thought processes. Anything and everything you learn at the university will be automatically stored, though other information will have to be manually added."

I'm frowning and shaking my head.

"What?"

"It's the most up to date technology."

"Technology? Chips? Chips are food. Potatoes, cut into strips, and fried in oil. They're a bit of a treat. They aren't tiny pieces of metal. And you never, ever allow metal to break the skin, it could cause all sorts of health issues." I might just be a village girl, but I'm not that stupid.

Kirela smiles again. "These will just slide straight in, you won't even be aware that they're there… after a day or two."

I shake my head again. "I'm not having anything inserted into my body."

Wulfrun reaches out to touch my elbow. "It's harmless, I promise. And it will be so helpful for you. And aside from the initial prick, it really doesn't hurt."

"No matter what you say, it's going to happen anyway, so if you sit still and be quiet we'll get through this so much faster, than if I have to call security to hold you down." Kirela has now inserted both thin strips of metal into some sort of needle, and watches me with her eyebrows raised.

I close my eyes, and sigh. This is probably some sort of mind control, but Kirela is right, I have no choice. If I do manage to run away, which is impossible right here, right now, the villagers will probably send me back anyway. And the idea of attending university does appeal. Studying something suggests a future, a life beyond the death I've been brought up to expect.

I nod, my eyes still squeezed shut, and I'm aware of Kirela coming behind me, her cool hand pulling back my hair as something sharp breaks the surface of my skin.

I wince, and then there's pressure as the two chips slide into my neck.

Then the needle has gone, my hair has fallen back, and I open my eyes to see everyone staring at me.

"How does that feel?" Tormod asks.

"Is it okay?"

"Did it hurt?" Ronther and Merric speak in unison.

I look around. "So, you are all speaking different languages, but you can understand each other?"

Everyone nods. "Isn't it wonderful?" Thyrius smiles. "It makes for much clearer communication. Far better than trying to interpret another person's words with your own limited knowledge of their language and culture. The device does it all for us."

I nod. "It does? Good. That... that is good."

Kirela smiles. "It is good. Now, we have one more thing before I will set you on your way. Your new home."

My heart races at her words. A new home. A home with five men. A home where I will be alone with five men. I swallow the lump in my throat, focusing on Kirela's assurance that rape is abhorrent to these creatures, as Kirela brings a screen down from the ceiling and gives us an address, and a virtual tour of the house.

It is huge. It has six bedrooms, and each bedroom has its own bathroom, complete with an indoor toilet and another separate room. There is a shared communal dining room and kitchen, and a very spacious living room.

I have never seen anything like it in my life. It is so different from the home I grew up in, a three-room dwelling where my parents slept in one room, my brothers and sisters and I in another, and we cooked and sheltered from the rain in the third. Every other moment of my life was spent outdoors. Why would anyone need a house this size?

Never in my wildest dreams of what living in the city might look like, did I imagine anything like this.

"There is a monorail direct to the university." I realise Kirela has been speaking again, and I've barely paid attention. "The stop is directly outside your front door. It's a short stroll to the shopping centre, and you have your own small garden, if you wish to grow any sorts of plants. The rooms are fully furnished, and we have provided you, Martha, with a basic wardrobe, however you men will have to have your belongings brought over." Kirela turned her attention back to me again.

"You have a small allowance, Martha, so if you wish to personalise your space in any way you will be able to do that. Each of these men have occupations, and their combined incomes will support you, until such time as you find employment, or, if you wish, once you have had a child, you are also welcome to stay at home to raise said child."

I nod. It's all a whirl. There's so much new information I've no idea how I'm going to remember it all, until I remember the hard drive chip in my neck.

Kirela said it was thought activated, so I give it a try.

Save information. I have option of working, or staying home with child.

There is a buzz, and then a soft female voice speaks in the back of my mind.

"Information saved."

I shudder. It's all just too strange. All I want to do is find my bed and sleep, and possibly hide away from the world for the next several months, while I get my head around it all.

Wulfrun links his arm through mine. "Shall we?"

I look at him, focus on those kind blue eyes, and take a deep breath. "Let's."

OUR HOME IS JUST as beautiful in real life as it was in the pictures. The men send me off to shower and change after my journey today, Wulfrun informing me he will cook me a decent meal.

After Kirela's comment that my village was too backward, I'm too embarrassed to admit I've never showered before, and I certainly don't want any of these men helping me, so I fumble with taps in the bathroom, surviving blasts of too hot water, and then too cold water, until a spray of just-right water shoots from a pipe emerging from the ceiling, filling the room with steam.

I leave my clothes on the floor, after retrieving the now very stale and squashed bread, crumbly cheese, and bruised apple from my pockets and placing them on a shelf in my room.

It feels like so much time has passed since I sat with Odran in the tree, and he gave me his backpack, and yet it's only been a day. There's a pang in my chest at the thought of him, and I wish I could've said goodbye to him. I wonder what he'll think when he learns I didn't run away? Will he think me foolish or brave? Will I ever see him again? If the situation ever arose, could I go back? Would I? And what would he do if he learnt I was still alive?

I dismiss that line of thought. Odran is in the past, and he has to stay there. Even if I escape from here, I can't go back to my village. I can't disrupt Dasha's future. I have to focus on surviving these first few days here, before I can decide what to do next.

I step into the shower. The water feels so nice on my back. There's a strong pressure behind it, and if I manoeuvre my body this way and that I can direct the water to all my aches and pains and have them massaged away.

There are bottles on the shelf, and I open them, various flowery scents filling the room. I've no idea exactly what these are for, but they are in the shower cubicle itself and so I imagine they must be to wash with, so I empty some out in my hand and rub it over my stomach, marvelling as the gel lathers up into bubbles.

I throw my head back, letting the water cascade over my face, loosing myself in the moment until a sharp knock brings me back to the present.

"Are you all right in there?" a voice calls, though I can't quite identify who is speaking over the noise of the water.

I twist the taps, stepping out onto the mat and wrapping myself in a soft towel.

"Yes, fine."

"Your meal is ready."

"Won't be long."

I rub my hair vigorously with the towel, and I drip water through the bedroom. There is no chest, so my clothes must be in the tall cupboards, but when I open them I'm not quite prepared for what I find.

There are half a dozen outfits, a couple of dresses, some skirts and slacks, blouses and sleeveless tops. They're beautiful – muted colours, nothing too bright, plain blues and greens and greys, some have patterns, some flower prints, some stripes.

It makes my own clothes look like rags, and I'm almost ashamed I wasn't given more beautiful clothes to wear to my 'sacrifice'. I guess being torn to shreds and devoured was considered a waste of good clothes, which wouldn't benefit the rest of the village. My farewell/birthday party had certainly not been for me.

By the time I emerge from my bedroom the men have given up waiting and are already half way through their meal. Only Wulfrun and Thyrius have their fully laden plates in front of them, and when I arrive Wulfrun stands to remove mine from the oven.

"I've kept it warm for you." He smiles as he carries it to the table, pulling out my chair so I can sit.

"You enjoyed your shower then?" Merric smirks at me, and I feel like the brunt of a bad joke.

"I did."

"You've never showered before." Wulfrun's gaze meets mine. His words are a statement not a question and I feel the blood rise in my cheeks.

"I've showered." None of these men need to know I've not. It's bad enough they think I'm unable to join in intelligent conversation.

"Okay." Wulfrun smiles at me, and returns to his meal. "I hope you like rabbit. We also have fresh greens from our garden—" he gestures towards the back yard. "—and some fresh vegetables from the market."

"It's delicious," I say, after taking my first bite. And it is, I've never tasted food so beautifully flavoured. "You're a very good cook."

Wulfrun beams at me. "Thank you."

"It's all right." Merric pokes at his food with a fork, before glancing up at me. "I have this one amazing dish though. You'll love it. I'll cook it for you sometime."

"That sounds great." I nod, and Wulfrun's smile fades. Surely he's not planning on doing all the cooking?

"So." Tormod looks at me. "First time in the big city, eh? We'll have to give you a tour sometime, head out to a few nightclubs and party!"

I have no idea what he's talking about, but from the way he speaks I'm not sure it's my thing. "Umm, yeah, sure."

"You don't have to do anything you don't want to." Wulfrun is watching me again, and a shiver travels my spine. Does he realise he's being more than a little bit creepy?

I force a smile. "That's fine. I'd love to try everything, at least once."

Wulfrun's eyes narrow, but he shrugs. "If you say so."

Ronther finishes first and pushes away from the table. "Sorry to leave so early, but I have work to do." He puts his dishes in the sink and leaves.

"Have you heard the date of the next general election has been set?" Thyrius asks the other men.

"I had," says Wulfrun. "It's too soon. They don't want to allow the opposition any chance of winning."

"Like it matters." Merric slides his chair back as he speaks. "It's not like one side is any different to the other."

The men break out into an argument about the pros and cons of each candidate. After the last several days it's all too much for me to handle, and I excuse myself and head to bed.

Thyrius rises from his chair as I do and nods a goodnight. "It is best to get a good night's sleep. Especially as you have your first day at University tomorrow."

I groan inwardly. Not even a day to adjust to this new lifestyle! I catch Wulfrun watching me again and force another smile. "That's right. Up bright and early. Good night all."

In my room there is a soft nightgown underneath my pillow, and I slide out of the perfectly clean clothes I've only just put on, pull the nightgown over my head, and slide into bed. Like the nightgown, the bed is so soft, the sheets so silky, it feels as though I must've been made a princess. I wonder how long it will be before they realise I don't deserve a life like this and send me back.

But then I put my head on the pillow and there's no room for other thoughts. I'm so tired I'm asleep in an instant.

CHAPTER 5

University is like nothing I ever expected. The first day we are thrust straight into the depths; history, sociology, and psychology. There are classes on politics, and some on philosophy, there's biological science, and agricultural science and lessons on public speaking, and debating, and essay and article writing.

I've never felt unintelligent before, but here, now, I feel so incredibly stupid.

Even things I am familiar with, like growing food and breeding animals, are presented using words I've never heard before. The idea that we could vote for our chief is something I just cannot get my head around. If we didn't like the way he did things we could just wait until the end of a prescribed time and vote in someone else seems too wonderful to be true, until someone points out that it only takes a few awful lies spread about a good leader and he would be voted out at the next election. And women can be leaders here, too.

Perhaps that would be the same in my own village, if there were more women. I'd like to think so.

The up side of all this strange new information is that I'm not the only one struggling with it. My classes are shared with close to twenty other women, all from poor villagers and towns, all some distance from the city. We're equally lacking in knowledge of this place and its ways.

"Do you think we will ever use any of this?" Dawn is seated next to me in every class, a quiet studious girl with dark hair and green eyes. "I mean, if we are here to produce babies, when will we get the chance to write essays on the current political climate or new historical theories?"

I shrug. "I've been told we can choose not to stay at home with the children."

Dawn frowns. "If we aren't caring for our children, who will?" It seems she was raised in a place where the women do most of the child-rearing, and she cannot possibly imagine a situation where someone else would look after her child.

I shrug again. "In my village it is often the grandmothers who care for the children. It frees up the women to do more work, because they are often more capable and faster than the older women, who have begun to slow down."

Dawn does not look convinced. "Do you see any grandmothers here?"

I don't, but I've only just been here a day, I'm sure there must be grandmothers somewhere. And having children is not something I want to worry about just yet. The one thing I have learnt in these first couple of days, is that consent is of the utmost importance here. I will not be forced to breed. And right now I have absolutely no intention of getting intimate with any men, let alone the ones I live with, so the question of who is going to look after my children is completely pointless.

After my first day at University I come home to what seems at first like an empty house. I realise that all the men have jobs, so I guess that's where they must be, but when I venture out into the garden to find some semblance of nature I find Wulfrun, tending the garden.

"You're home!" His smile is wide, and there's a sparkle in his eyes that I can't deny is quite attractive. Still, I push that thought aside. If I never agree to sex, I'll never fall pregnant, and maybe they'll get sick of me and set me loose, so I can make a home somewhere else.

"How was your day?"

I tell him a bit about my day, the lessons, and the women I've met.

"That's fantastic. It's always great to make friends. It always helps people to settle in, if they can make friendships quickly."

I give a slight smile, I'm not sure what to say to that.

"Don't worry about the studies too much, okay? It feels huge now, but you'll get the hang of it, and if you ever need help with anything, there are five of us here, all more than happy to help."

I frown. "I never said I was having trouble."

He reaches out to tap my shoulder. "I can read body language, Martha. You don't have to say anything, I know what you're thinking."

My mouth drops open in surprise as my whole face seems to burn up. "You, what?"

He shrugs. "I can tell when people are telling the truth. Like last night. I know you've never experienced a shower before. I'm not sure why you feel it's something to be ashamed of. Most women we bring in from the outlying villages haven't, but if you don't want the others to know, I won't tell them."

I'm too shocked to say anything, so Wulfrun continues. "Truth is such an important part of any relationship. You must never be ashamed of it. We can all learn from each other, if only we tell the truth."

"I, but… I—" I don't know what to say. "I've had a busy few days. I need to lie down."

He nods. "It can be confronting to people. That's okay. You have a rest. You'll feel better afterwards, I'm sure."

I DON'T THINK I'll actually sleep, but eventually I do,

ONE GIRL FIVE HUNGRY BEASTS

and when I wake it's to the noise of laughing and chatter from the shared room.

I brush my hair, take a deep breath and put on a brave face.

"You're awake!" Merric is standing in the doorway to the kitchen, so he is the first to see me. He strides down the hallway, enveloping me in a hug. "You're looking well for someone who's been thrust into a completely alien world." He grins, and I have the feeling I'm supposed to laugh at that, but I don't. He gestures to the kitchen. "Wulfrun is still cooking dinner. Do you like video games?"

I raise an eyebrow. "I don't even know what a video game is."

His grins widens. "Then it's well past time you learned."

He grabs my hand, dragging me into the shared lounge and over to the couch. I sit down, watching while he connects cables into a large black panel on the wall, and then thrusts some sort of device into my hands that matches the one he holds.

Thyrius enters the room. "Oh Merric! You're not going to force the poor girl to suffer through your games, are you? At least give her a chance to socialise before thrusting this on her."

He sits in the chair next to me, turning to catch my gaze. "I can't imagine you've ever come across these where you're from, but I can assure it's a complete waste of time."

Merric snorts. "Creative play is *never* a waste of

time."

Thyrius raises an eyebrow. "That is not creative. This is creative." He pulls a small guitar from beside the seat and holds my gaze as he begins to strum. It sounds beautiful, but then he starts to sing, and when I hear his first words I blush and have to look away.

"My beautiful Martha," he sings. "What a gift you are."

Merric laughs.

"Looks like your idea of creative is not appreciated right now, Thyrius."

Thyrius ignores Merric, and continues to strum and sing, but I'm so embarrassed that he's making up a song about me, right here and now.

Merric pushes a button on the panel, and I watch as it flickers, a small image growing from a dot in the centre of the screen.

A few words scroll up the screen, and then a picture jumps up, two werewolves, one with a bow, the other with a sword. Both have packs on their backs and strange clothing on their furry bodies.

Merric pushes a button on his device and instructs me to do the same.

"You select your character here. You can pick between a warrior, a witch, and a healer, and if you want you can change face shape and fur colour and all that sort of stuff."

I select a healer. I watch Merric first, then flick through the options for my own character. I really have no idea about any of it, so in the end I just select whatever option is in front of me, just to get things moving.

"Great choice!"

There's a chuckle from the doorway and I glance up to see Wulfrun watching me. He can tell I've no idea what I'm doing. I turn my attention back to Merric and the screen. Our characters are standing side-by-side in a lush green forest, which looks so real I feel like I'm looking through a window.

"Okay, so, you move your character like this—" He points to some buttons on my device, "—and you attack enemies like this. Normally I skip the tutorial, but we'll start with that now, so you can get the hang of how it works, and then we can move on to a proper level."

It takes forever to get through the tutorial, and then we only manage it because Merric's character saves me at every single turn. I feel useless, following his character through the game as he takes out every enemy and casts healing spells over me every time my health gets low, which seems to happen often.

Merric doesn't seem to notice that, though. "Fantastic! We can move onto round one!"

"I'm not much of a healer," I say, my face burning.

"Ah, you'll be fine. Just takes a while to get the hang of it, that's all."

I set the device down on the couch between us and shake my head. "I don't think I'm ready to move on to the real game. I really didn't do very well."

"You were fine, I'll help you, you'll get the hang of it in no time."

I shake my head. "Thanks, Merric. But I've had a huge day, and I really don't think I picked up much. Maybe another time, when I'm not so tired."

Merric's face drops, but he shrugs. "Sure. Another time. No worries."

I stand up and walk out into the hallway, only to bump into Tormod.

"There you are!" His smile is so wide I think his face might crack. "I've bought you a gift." He's holding out his hand, a small box sitting on his open palm. "Go on, take it. It won't hurt."

I'm really too tired to be dealing with this right now, and I'm actually feeling really wary of people bringing unexpected gifts. I've never known a surprise gift to actually be anything nice, well except perhaps from Odran, but he hardly counts.

I take the box from Tormod and pull on the ribbon. The box falls open and inside is a tiny carving of a bird.

"It's a welcome swallow. To welcome you here, see." He's gazing intently at me, and I force a smile. "That's really lovely, Tormod."

"You like it?"

I nod, ever so thankful it's not Wulfrun standing across from me. "It's really lovely," I repeat. "I'll put it somewhere safe in my room."

Tormod's grin widens even further, and I turn to see Thyrius standing in the doorway to his room, his eyes narrowed. I scurry back to the bedroom, ever so grateful to be able to lock the door behind me.

I don't know whether Tormod will ever see inside my room, but I figure I'd better put his bird somewhere visible, just in case, so I set it on the window sill behind my bed. At least then I won't have to look at it all the time.

I think about having a shower, but there's a knock at my door, and Wulfrun's voice calls through.

"Dinner's ready!"

"Coming." I take a deep breath, and prepare myself for another onslaught of conversation.

Though I'm worn out from study, I'm ever so grateful to be able to use it as an excuse to leave the table early.

Once again Thyrius stands as I do, and this time so does Ronther, offering to help me with my study as he takes my plates to the sink.

I can't very well say no, and soon we are sitting together at his desk, in the office off his bedroom.

I go over what I remember from the day, frustrated when I find I can't remember much at all.

"You have a memory chip, Martha. I know you're not used to it yet, but it will be so helpful for you. Don't forget to use it."

I sigh. What was it Kirela said about the chip? Everything I learn at University is stored automatically.

"Okay." I take a deep breath, and think about my first lesson of the day, which happened to be philosophy. *What did I learn?*

There's a soft whirring, which I really dislike, and then that soft female voice begins to speak.

"Introduction to Philosophy. The class began with—" The voice continues, rattling off all the information my professor shared with the class this morning.

"Wow." I blink, as she finishes. "That is weird, but really helpful."

Ronther smiles. "It makes everything so much easier – every piece of information you've been taught is all there on hand. You might have to be a bit more specific when you ask a question though, otherwise you'll have her rattling off for hours on end."

I laugh. "I'll remember that."

It doesn't take long for me to go over all of the day's learning now I've figured out how the memory chip works, and Ronther is right, everything is so much easier. But there are still words and concepts I don't understand. Ronther is fantastic at explaining everything so clearly and concisely, that by the end of our session, I feel like I've emerged from a fog.

"That is fantastic." I'm beaming at him, I'm so relieved that I understand the day's lectures now. "I really appreciate it."

He smiles back, though he only holds my gaze for a short time, glancing away as his cheeks begin to turn red. "I suspect you have a few readings to do before tomorrow," he says, standing up. "If there's anything you don't understand, come knock on my door, anytime of day or night. I'd be more than happy to help."

I give him a warm smile. "Thanks. I'll do that."

CHAPTER 6

The following days continue much the same. University is a barrage of information. I spend my lunch breaks with Dawn and the other women, trying desperately to understand everything we've been taught and make sense of this society that really is so alien from what we know.

Ronther's explanations are so helpful, that I'm able to explain concepts from the previous days' lectures so that everyone understands, and soon our lunch times become an unofficial study session, every one discussing the topics in between eating the delicious meals in the university café.

At home Wulfrun cooks a delicious meal every night, Merric is desperate to teach me how to play his computer games, Ronther helps me with my studies, and Tormod brings me more presents. By the end of the week my window sill is cluttered with tiny birds and animals, each with some meaning special only to Tormod.

Thyrius sings. He doesn't only sing, he also plays a flute, and a harp, and a very small guitar, but mostly he sings, sweet songs about love and loss and beautiful women and what a gift they are.

At first I thought he just liked to sing, but then I realised that he only does it around me. If I come across him unexpectedly he's never singing, he never has his guitar with him when it's just him and the other men hanging out, he never sings in front of them, either. He only starts up when he realises I'm home and nearby. Sometimes he sits outside my bedroom door, strumming his guitar, humming tunes under his breath. It's weird, and my face flushes every time he starts, which just seems to encourage him to sing some more.

By the end of the first week I'm trying to find ways to avoid him. I begin to spend more time at University, forming a study group with some of the women, or deliberately missing the mono-rail so I have to wait for the next one.

I discover that Dawn lives fairly close to me, only a block or two further on, and when she invites me to walk home with her one afternoon I'm quick to accept.

She's mostly quiet, and we enjoy the scenery, most of which I've missed in the monorail, which is set several metres into the air. It travels so fast I soon feel ill if I look out the window.

"Do your men, sort of, woo you?" Dawn giggles, as though she's nervous or scared to be thought a fool.

I glance at her, my eyes wide. "I didn't think of it like that, but now you mention it, I think that is what they're doing. Wulfrun cooks every night. He won't let anyone else in the kitchen, not even to cook for themselves, he's so possessive of it. He and Thyrius always wait until I'm seated before they eat, and they're always rushing to be the first to pull my chair out for me when I sit down. They pretend like they haven't been fighting when I enter the room, but I can often hear them up the hallway, pushing each other aside to get to the chair. And Thyrius sings. If I can sneak into my room without him realising I'm home he never sings. But the moment he realises I'm home he's humming under his breath or singing aloud, or worse, hanging about outside my door, playing songs. It's so embarrassing! Ronther is the only one who treats me as an equal, the only time we interact is when I'm studying with him, mostly anyway. Merris insists on playing this god-awful computer game. And Tormod brings me a present every day, tiny little figurines of animals and flowers."

Dawn's eyes are wide. "Mine too! Well, the cooking, and the singing, and the gifts. Not figurines, but flowers and sweets and jewellery. When Guthram learnt I like to draw he bought me a sloped table and paper and the finest pencils I've ever seen in my life, and he's paid for someone to come and give me art lessons at the house every afternoon." She shakes her head. "It's all too much. I've never been given anything like that in my life."

"Wow. At least those things are useful, though. I don't know what I'm supposed to do with all these little birds and animals. They're taking up every available shelf space, and it just looks so untidy!"

"What are they made of?"

I shrug. "Wood, I guess."

"Perhaps you could put them in the garden? You could set some of the birds in the trees, and hide some of the other animals under plants. When you do have children, they'll be delighted to find little creatures in the garden."

"You sound like you have experience there."

Dawn shrugs. "It's what my older brother used to do for me. He'd whittle small creatures and hide them in the woods, and then pretend to discover them when we were out walking."

I feel a stab of jealousy and push it aside. "Sounds like you got on well with your brother."

Dawn nods, a wistful smile on her face. "He was great. He'd always watch out for me. He told me that he'd protect me for as long as he possibly could, and that when the werewolves took me, he'd come and find me."

"You didn't think you were going to die?"

"Die?" Dawn shakes her head. "No. Did you?"

I shrug. "We never knew what was going to happen to the girls who were sacrificed. So, everyone said that they were eaten." I kick at a pebble and watch it skitter across the path.

"Oh, Martha!" Dawn reaches out to touch my arm. "That must have been terrible! You were so brave to face that!"

I shrug. "I had no choice. I thought about running away. The day before the sacrifice my friend, Odran, brought me some supplies so I *could* run away. He had several days' worth of food. And believe me, I seriously considered it, but I didn't know what would happen if I wasn't at the sacrifice point. The werewolves might've taken my sister instead, or maybe they would've just destroyed the entire village and killed Odran."

Dawn's eyes are wide. "You're a very good person, Martha. So selfless. Much better than me."

"What are you talking about?"

"I would've fled the moment Odran handed me the bag. If I honestly thought I was going to die, I would've been out of there."

I look at her. "What did you believe was going to happen?"

She shrugs, her cheeks colouring. "I knew we were going to be bred. I don't know how my village knew, but that's what I was taught, that my sacrifice would save the village from poverty and I would be taken somewhere where I would be fed and sheltered, and I would carry werewolf babies until I couldn't anymore."

"Is this what you imagined when you thought of

what was to come?" I wave a hand to indicate our surroundings.

Dawn shakes her head. "This is paradise compared to my expectations. I thought I would be chained up somewhere, available whenever the men wanted to have a go." Her voice breaks and I reach out to touch her elbow. She glances at me and I see there are tears in her eyes. "Most of the girls in our village are protected. If they're damaged in any way, it reduces the amount of money the parents can ask for in the dowry. But the first-born daughters in our village are considered a fair-go for anyone. As long as they pulled out, so I didn't fall pregnant, any boy or man, or group of them, could take me and no one would say a word."

"Oh, Dawn." I reach out and wrap my arms around her, and she drops her head onto my shoulder, quietly sobbing. I had thought my life was terrible, but really, I had it easy.

"Didn't that make you want to run away?" I can't imagine how Dawn coped with that life. I can't imagine how I would have survived, if that were me.

She pulls away, wiping her eyes with the back of her sleeve. "I thought it would be the same wherever I went, that I would always be at the beck and call of men. But I watched enough of the mothers in my village to know that once a woman is pregnant, her husband doesn't go near her until after the baby is born. I figured there would be at least nine-months of being left alone, and if I fell pregnant straight away every time then I would only need to be with a man once or twice a year."

I shake my head, and we walk in silence for a while, as I try to absorb everything she's said to me.

"So, what will you do here? Now you know you'll never be touched without your consent. You need never be with a man again."

Dawn shakes her head, her lower lip trembling. "I want a daughter. I've always wanted a daughter, and now I am here I know she'll be safe – she'll never be a sacrifice like I was. But to have a daughter..." She looks away and sighs.

"To have a daughter you have to lie with a man."

She nods.

"Perhaps it will be easier, with time? We've only been here a week, perhaps once you know them better you might be attracted to one of them."

She glances at me. "Are you?"

I think of Wulfrun, but push the thought away. He's physically attractive, but he's still a werewolf. "No." I shake my head. "I have no intention of sleeping with any of them. But I don't want children, either, so that's not something I ever need to worry about."

I hear shouting as we turn down a side street, and I see a huge crowd at the end, werewolves in wolf form, mixed with human-looking people. I still haven't learnt how to tell the difference between a wolf in human form and an actual human, and I don't even know if it's possible to do so.

I grab Dawn's arm and pull back.

"Maybe we should go another way?"

She shakes her head. "It's fine. It's just the arena."

"The arena?"

Dawn peers at me. "Haven't you heard of it?"

"No."

"It's where the Werewolves go to sort out their issues. If one wolf has a problem with another wolf he challenges him to a fight, and unless the other wold can find a loophole, he has to accept the challenge." Dawn crinkles her nose. "It's all very bloody."

"You've seen a few, then?"

She nods. "I walk home every day. This is the quickest route. The first day there weren't any fights, just a big empty arena." She laughs. "I wondered what it was for, isn't that silly? It's so obvious now, but the next day when I turned down the street and saw such a mass of people, I was terrified. I didn't think I was going to make it home."

I can see why she thought that. We near the crowd, large enough to block off the street and chanting so loudly I can barely hear Dawn when she suggests we slink along the back wall to get past.

It's a bit of an effort to get through the crowd, but once we manage it Dawn suggests we climb a scaffold, to get a look at the fight.

"You've got to see it at least once," she says.

I don't see why, but I follow her anyway. The arena turns out to be a large round hole, dug down at least two metres below ground-level. There's a fence around the top, and up above them, a huge screen showing the fight below, for those who can't get close enough to see it themselves.

The fighting is vicious, one wolf already has several gashes across his face and chest as his opponent flashes his claws and brings them across the first wolf's stomach. There's a bit more parrying, as the first wolf lands a few punches and scratches, and manages to knock the second wolf over, but when the second wolf raises his hind legs and kicks full force into the first wolf's stomach I can see the first wolf has no hope of winning.

"They're not going to kill each other, are they?" I ask Dawn, who seems to know a bit about it.

She shakes her head. "It's just a battle until one can't get up anymore. Sometimes one of them decides it's not worth it and gives up quickly, others seem to find reserves to keep the fight going for ages."

"How do you know so much already?"

"Guthram, one of my werewolves, explained it to me, after that first fight. He's been very helpful in teaching me everything about this place." She begins the climb back down to the street. "Like I said, you've got to see it once, and then you don't have to see it ever again. But the bonus is that you know exactly what anyone is talking about when they mention the arena, so you don't seem completely naïve."

"Right," I say again, nodding my head. That does make some sort of sense. There's so much to learn about this place, and it seems university is not necessarily going to teach us all we need to know.

I wonder briefly if any of my werewolves fight in the arena, but then I shake my head. None of them seem to be the aggressive type. I can't imagine any of them fighting at all, let alone in something like that.

CHAPTER 7

I open the door to a mixture of cheering and boo-ing from the shared lounge.

"What's happening here?" I ask.

"There you are!" Merric turns to me. "You're late! We thought you might've heard of Ronther's big fight and gone to support him."

"Ronther's fight?"

Merric gestures at the screen, and I realise that I'm looking at the arena, the same two wolves I was watching, still at each other. The first wolf has even more injuries, and he's staggering across the arena, barely able to stand up.

My mouth drops open. "Is one of those wolves Ronther?"

Merric grins. "Certainly is. Getting pounded!"

"What?"

He must see my concern because he shrugs. "He'll

be all right. He's tough. He'll bounce back."

Wulfrun is watching us, as always. "More to the point, Merric," he says. "If Ronther's out of action Martha might have more time to spend with you."

Merric scowls, but I ignore him. "Why is he fighting?"

Wulfrun shrugs. "Some dispute over land, I think. I guess we'll find out sooner or later."

On the screen the badly injured werewolf, *Ronther*, I remind myself, is knocked down yet again. This time it takes him a moment to push himself up off the ground.

"Is Ronther badly hurt?"

Wulfrun shrugs. "Hard to say until they get a doctor to look at him. To be fair, Merric is right, Ronther should be okay. Sometimes things go awry and aren't easily fixed, but werewolves are good healers. Usually everything is okay."

Usually.

I hold on to Wulfrun's words, surprised to find I'm actually worried about Ronther, a werewolf I've known for only a fortnight.

Of all of them, he's been the least pushy. Helping me with my studies when I need it, happy to go back to his own work when I tell him I'm fine. He doesn't loiter around my bedroom door, or watch every movement I make, or bring me these useless trinkets, or force me to play video games I'm fairly certain I will never understand.

It's late in the evening when we finally get news,

Ronther delivered to our house in a wheelchair by his doctor, who informs us that while Ronther has a lot of injuries, it's not worth the cost of the hospital to keep him there. As long as someone regularly changes his bandages and reapplies some healing ointment, he should be back to his usual self within a few days.

The doctor's words lift a huge weight from my shoulders, and I have to blink away tears of relief before anyone else sees them.

"Okay." I smile at Ronther, still in wolf form, whose eyes seem to be glazed over from some medication or another. "Guess we'd better get you into bed, then."

"We can all help with that, Martha." It's Wulfrun, watching me intently again, *still!* He seems hurt, surely it cannot be because of my attention to Ronther?

The other men take charge, pushing the chair up the hall to Ronther's room, then each helping to lift him in to bed, while I pull the covers up over his shoulders.

He winces, and I pull my hands away, but before I can apologise his eyes are closed, a slight snore coming from his mouth. I smile. He's kinda sweet like this, vulnerable and dependent, even in wolf-form. I shake my head. That sort of thinking has to stop!

When I come out of my room Thyrius is there in the hallway, strumming his guitar and humming softly to himself. When he sees me his eyes light up, and he begins to sing.

"Oh lovely Martha, oh Martha, my love—"

I put up a hand. "Stop, please."

His face falls and I feel awful, but I really can't stand being sung to like this. Of all the things the men do, his is the most obvious, and it draws attention to us both, every time.

"You don't like being serenaded?"

I shake my head. "I'm sorry. It's lovely, really. You play well, and you're a fine singer. But it brings everyone's attention onto us, and it makes me feel really uncomfortable."

"Oh." He lets go of the guitar so it hangs on the strap around his neck. "I was doing it for you. I thought women liked being sung to."

I shake my head. "Not all women."

"Right. I'm sorry. I didn't intend to make you feel uncomfortable."

He strides past me down the hall, clearly offended. Perhaps I should have just let him play? But I push that thought aside, along with the guilt. I shouldn't have to put up with something I don't like, just because someone else thinks I should like it.

THE NEXT DAY I skip University—I'm not going anywhere until I know Ronther's okay—and instead I collect up all of Tormod's presents into a basket and take them out into the garden.

Wulfrun's out there, weeding a patch, and I see he's dug a new section of garden and planted out several different types of vegetables.

When the door clicks shut behind me he glances up, a frown on his face.

"You're not going to University today?"

I shake my head. "I have to keep an eye on Ronther."

Wulfrun raises an eyebrow. "I can look after Ronther. Your studies are important."

I shrug. "Ronther is exceptionally good at helping me study, so I'm sure he can help me catch up when he's better, if I need to. I doubt I'll miss much."

I take a small walk around the garden, actually looking for the first time at all the different trees and shrubs. There are a few fruit trees, apple and pear mostly, some raspberry canes, and a semi-tamed mess of blackberry bramble. At the opposite end of the garden where Wulfrun is, are several flowering plants, their scent attracting the bees so the plants almost seem alive with all the movement around them.

"What are you up to?" Wulfrun asks, still kneeling in the garden.

"Nothing much." I purse my lips trying to see where I could place these animals.

"What have you got there?" He stands, peering into my basket.

"Just a few knick knacks. Thought I might decorate the garden with them."

He raises an eyebrow, his gaze on me. Then he frowns. "They're the gifts Tormod has given you, aren't they? you don't want them, and so you're going to litter my garden with his rubbish."

I shake my head. "They're not rubbish, they just need a proper home. And being animals and birds and flowers, I figured that the garden was the best home they could have."

"No." Wulfrun has his hands on his hips now. "I'll not have those things in my garden."

I find the perfect tree for one of the birds, and jam its little feet into the fork of a branch.

"It's not just *your* garden, Wulfrun. And *those things* are my presents. I can put my presents wherever I feel the need. Besides, it'll be fun for the children when they come along."

That catches him, but only for a moment. "You forget, Martha. I can read your body language. You don't want children. You still don't want any of us to even touch you, though Ronther's injury is helping him work away at that particular barrier. These aren't for the children, they're so you can offload them and still feel good about yourself."

I place the figurines around the garden as he talks, humming a little tune and ignoring him. I realise suddenly the tune is one of Thyrius' and want to stop, but don't want Wulfrun to read anything into that. But now I turn, my eyes narrowed.

"You may think you know everything, but maybe you don't. Maybe you just make assumptions and then think you are so much better than everyone else and so of course, your assumptions must be right. Well I know something about you right now. You're jealous. Jealous of Ronther, and jealous of Tormod. You want no sign of any of your rivals in this garden. But you know what? This isn't your garden. This is our garden. You are one of five men who I somehow am supposed to spread my attention around, all the while trying to learn how to live in this society. So maybe you need to just suck it up and stop being a know-it-all arsehole."

I've bottled up my frustrations and anger for so long, his cocky know-it-all attitude is the last straw. Wulfrun's mouth drops open, his eyes wide. I smile to myself, the relief that I've finally stood up to him flooding my body with adrenalin.

"I'm going to go inside now and tend to Ronther's wounds. And tonight, I am going to cook dinner. Or maybe I'll get Merric to do it, seeing as he's been banging on about that one great dish he can do. The kitchen isn't yours, and the garden isn't yours, and I am not yours. It's about time you realised that."

I flounce back inside, striding up the hall to stop outside Ronther's door and take a few deep breaths to calm myself before barging in.

When I do, he's awake, sitting up in bed with a grin on his face.

"Wow, Martha. I never knew you had it in you."

My face flushes. "You heard that?"

"Every word. And I'm so proud of you. About

time someone stood up to Mr Blunt."

I laugh. "I don't think he does it to be annoying, it's just who he is." I realise that I'm getting a bit of a soft spot for Wulfrun, too. *Damn!* "Would be nice if he was a bit more self-aware, though." I add, glancing at Ronther to see if he noticed.

"Tell me about it," he says, apparently unaware. Then again, this is Ronther I'm talking to, not Wulfrun, not the wolf-man who picks up everything. "The man has no idea when he's crossing boundaries. Though I'm not sure he'd care if he was." Ronther's chuckle is stopped short by a wince, and I move closer to the bed to see how I can help.

"A bit more of that pain relief would do wonders," he says, pointing to the bottle of medicine on the table.

I read the instructions and measure out his required dose.

"I'll need to change those bandages now," I say, taking the clean bandages and dressing from the bag of bits and pieces the doctor left.

"If you must." He grins, as he raises one arm, so I can get to his bandages more easily.

I undo the small clip that fastens his bandages, and slowly and carefully wind the bandages back around his body. I know Ronther's putting on a brave face, but even so he winces several times and I realise just how much he was hurt in the fight.

"Why did you do it?" I ask, applying the ointment onto the wounds on his chest.

"I didn't have a choice." He takes a sharp intake of breath when the ointment touches his sores and continues to speak through gritted teeth.

"I had land, passed to me by my uncle. But that other wolf had a claim to it as well. I didn't want to give it up, and neither did he, so he challenged me to a duel. Once the challenge is thrown, there's no backing down. Even if I wanted to I couldn't have. Believe me, I would rather just handed the land over than get in a physical fight for it. So I went to fight. I never ever imagined he'd challenge me, and when he did I never thought he'd follow through with it. We went to school together, and he was always such a weakling. I guess he's trained a lot since then." Ronther shakes his head. "I don't think I've trained at all since school. Much prefer books to anything too physical."

I smile. "Well I'm glad you've gone down the book track. I'd be completely lost if it wasn't for you. I don't think University is really the place for me."

He reaches out, wincing again, to take my hand. "You've got the head for it," he says. "Just not the practise. It'll come in time, you just need to persevere with it."

I give his hand a squeeze, pretending not to notice when he pretends he didn't just wince, yet again.

"Don't you heal faster when you're sleeping? I should let you have a rest."

Ronther shakes his head. "I'll heal fast enough. But you're missing a day of Uni, just for me. How about you bring your books in and we can go over the readings for today's lectures?"

There's no way I'm going to refuse that, so I duck into my room to gather my books. I spend the rest of the day with Ronther, reading aloud passages from my text books, listening to him explain all the ins and outs of each subject, ever so grateful when he can give me an easily understood definition of the many words that I stumble on.

By the end of the day my brain feels like mush, and yet I feel like I've learnt so much more than a usual day at Uni would teach me.

"Perhaps you just need to teach me here at home." I'm joking, but only just. How much better would it be if I didn't have to stutter through wrong answers for my lecturers? Ronther is so patient, imagine how fast I'd learn if he could take over. He did a far better job at teaching me than any of the lecturers at the University had, so far, anyway.

"That would be fantastic!" He grins. "I'd certainly enjoy it. Unfortunately, I've never been qualified as a teacher, so there's no way that would be allowed. But I can still tutor you in the afternoons and on weekends. I'm here for you, Martha. Whenever you need anything, and I do mean anything at all, you only have to ask."

He rests his hand on my knee, and though I can't see anything even remotely suggestive in his eyes, I have the sudden sense that he is talking about sexual needs.

A shiver travels my body, and I rub my arms.

"It's starting to get a bit cold, now." I put my hand over his, and give it a friendly squeeze as I remove it from my knee and place it back on the bed.

"I'm going to grab a jacket, maybe see how the other guys are doing."

He smiles, but it seems forced, and I'm certain I'm not imagining the disappointment in his eyes.

"Sure, no worries." His stomach grumbles. "Tell Wulfrun to hurry up with dinner!"

I realise at his words that I told Wulfrun to stay out of the kitchen tonight, so that I or Merric could cook. But I haven't spoken to Merric all day, and now it's almost dinner time. I'll have to find something, though I have no idea exactly what these werewolves like to eat, or even what ingredients we have in the cupboard.

I race into the kitchen, so worried about what I might feed everyone with that I'm not even vaguely aware of the delicious scent wafting down the hall.

It's only when I reach the kitchen and see Wulfrun at the stove that the smell registers, and I realise he has another delicious meal almost ready to go.

"Oh." I stop when I see him, and he glances at me.

"I know you said not to be here," he gives me a sheepish grin, "but the time when someone needed to have dinner on the stove was passing, and you were tending to Ronther, and I couldn't find Merric, so I thought I should get something started. We all need to eat, after all."

I'm speechless, for the briefest moment.

"Wow. Thank you, Wulfrun. You didn't have to do that, especially after what I said to you this morning. I really appreciate it. I got so caught up with Ronther, that I lost track of time—"

"No worries at all, Martha." Wulfrun shakes his head, as he removes something hot and steaming from the oven. "You have nothing to apologise for. I understand that sometimes I speak when it would be better not to. So, I apologise for that. And I want you to know, I'm here to help. Truly. If ever you need anything at all, just ask."

I find myself backing out of the room, his words echoing Ronther's much too closely. Anything at all. Everyone is here for me. Except that's not true, is it? I'm here for them, I'm here so they can ease their sexual frustration, and every little thing they do is aimed at just one thing. Getting inside my pants.

Do they think that a woman's libido is just a constantly running machine that needs fulfillment from where ever she can get it? Maybe some women are like that, but not me. I'm too aware of the fact that sex is something that is going to impose on my personal space, and be messy, and lead to all sorts of unpleasant expectations of repeat performances. I'm not ready for a first time, yet, with one of them. Let alone repeat performances with several.

I force a smile.

"Guess I'll go see what everyone else is up to."

CHAPTER 8

*E*veryone else is scattered around the house. Merric is playing his video games as usual, but I manage to peek around the door without him seeing me, so he doesn't call me to play yet another round of trailing-after-Merric's-character-as-he-does-amazing-things. It wouldn't be so bad if he actually let me lead now and again, but I'm so sick of being told which answers to select in the pre-programmed conversations, or what order I should do things in. Maybe Merric has played it enough to know what works best in the long run, but following step by step instructions makes it so boring! I just want to explore myself, and see what some of these other answers and paths might lead to.

Thyrius and Tormod are out in the garden, examining the presents scattered around the yard.

"You've put my creatures in the garden," Tormod says when he sees me.

I nod. I'm not sure whether he's angry or pleased.

"I just thought they'd brighten the place up, and they're animals after all. They belong outdoors, not cramped in my room."

"They're not real." Thyrius is smiling at me, and I laugh.

"I know they're not real. But this seemed like a nicer place to put them. And then we can all enjoy them, too."

Tormod is smiling. "It is a nicer spot for them," he agrees. "I wish I'd thought of it myself." He comes over to take my hand. "I've hidden a new one for you, somewhere over here." He leads me over to a large tree. "Can you find it?"

My eyes widen. I'm not entirely sure I took enough notice of either the figurines themselves, or where I put them in the garden, to be certain of discovering a new one amongst the plants. I walk slowly around the base of the tree, checking out the couple of birds I know I put there, and the few animals I hid underneath.

Tormod's grin is growing, and I sense that he actually really likes this game of hide and seek. Is he pleased to be outsmarting me? I hope that's the case. It will save a lot of angst if so.

I lift some of the branches of the lower shrubs, and peek in the little nooks and crannies created by the tree's roots.

Nothing *looks* new. What about that little rabbit? I give it a quick glance. If I look too long and it's not the one he'll know I have no idea what he's given me, and that will hurt him. No. I remember that one on my windowsill, one of the earliest ones he'd given me.

I glance at Tormod, who looks particularly pleased with himself, and so I take a risk and stand up, arms spread.

"I can't find it, you've hidden it too well."

"Knew it!" He's honestly gleeful, like a little child. "Right, over, here." He takes a few steps behind me, and points to a small snake, curled and coiled around a thin branch, not on the tree I was searching, but on a low bush behind me.

"I never said it was on the tree," he says. "I said it was over this area. You'll have to do better next time."

I grin, relieved to not have offended him. I make a mental note to come out and examine all these figurines when he's not home, so that next time we play I can be certain of what is new and what is old.

Behind Tormod, Thyrius' eyes are narrowed.

Wulfrun calls out that dinner is ready, and I'm not sure I've ever felt so grateful, but inside there's a tension in the air.

"Seems Martha likes my creatures." Tormod speaks directly to Wulfrun. "She's hidden them, all over your garden."

My ears prick. "What? That's not just Wulfrun's garden. That's everyone's garden."

Wulfrun answers me, though his gaze never leaves Tormod. "One of the things you haven't picked up about werewolves, Martha. We're territorial, it doesn't matter how small the territory, once we've claimed it, it's ours."

"That's right." Tormod nods. "And Wulfrun thought that by claiming the largest space in the house, he'd also be able to claim the largest part of your heart. Shame that's failed, isn't it Wulfy."

Wulfrun's eyes narrow. "Trouble is, *Tormy*, the creatures aren't there because she's bringing your things into my territory, it's because she doesn't want them in her own."

I feel my face burn, but Tormod doesn't even seem to notice. "You say whatever you need to feel good about yourself, Wulfrun. We all know the truth here."

Thyrius clears his throat. "The truth is, that the two of you are exceedingly jealous, not just of each other, but of Ronther, I dare say."

He glances at me. "How is Ronther, by the way?"

I can't help but feel that Thyrius is actually asking a very different question, and I wonder what the best answer would be. "He seems to be healing fast."

Thyrius nods. "I presume that all the attention you're giving him will make him heal exceedingly fast."

I frown. "I don't understand."

"All day, in his rooms. I didn't think bandages took quite that long to change. Though I suppose he does have a lot of them. Shame he wasn't tougher, then none of us would have to be losing time with you."

My frown deepens. "I took my University work in with me. Ronther was helping me with my studies."

"I'm sure he was."

Now I shake my head. "He's too injured for anything else."

Merric raises an eyebrow. "So you did try?"

"Try what? No!"

"Then why didn't you want to sit with me this afternoon. I saw you peak in. But you were gone before I had the chance to say anything. Too ashamed to face me because you'd done Ronther before me."

I stand up, my chair falling to the ground behind me.

"You're all a bunch of jealous arseholes. 'Werewolves have territory', what bullshit! If that's the case then you need to change this whole system you've got going here, because I am nobody's 'territory', and I won't be claimed or owned. I haven't *done* any of you, and if you continue to carry on like a bunch of immature children I'll have absolutely no desire to ever *do* any of you, at all!" My hands are clenched by my sides, and I'm panting as I make eye contact with each one of them. But now I squeeze my eyes shut. "I just wish I could go home!"

Wulfrun sniggers, and I turn to glare at him.

"What's so funny?" I ask, my eyes narrowed.

He stands and meets my gaze, eye to eye. "This is your home. It's the only semblance to a home you've ever had. You've never been loved anywhere else. I can see it in the way you treat yourself. You scurry here and there, desperate to avoid attention. You don't think yourself worthy of gifts, or songs, or even someone's time." His dark shaggy hair has fallen over his eyes, but he doesn't flinch, and the certainty in his blue eyes in overwhelming.

"You don't love yourself, because you've never been loved. You think you don't deserve everything we are trying to do for you, you're constantly seeing an ulterior motive, even when there isn't one." He pauses for effect. "Some people, werewolves included, are just nice people. Some people, when thrust together in a situation that is not of their choosing, will actually do their best to make things as easy as possibly for those around them. In fact, I would be so bold as to say that *most* people are actually that way inclined, that there are few in this world who are only in it for themselves. And even though I don't always get along with my fellow werewolves sitting at this table, I would say that we are all just trying to make the best of an unfortunate situation." Now Wulfrun's eyes are narrowed at me, all his anger and frustration directed my way.

"The problem is, that you don't know about nice people because you've never experienced any. As far as your parents were concerned you were nothing but a source of riches. All they had to do was keep you safe for the first twenty years of your life. Then they'd be rich beyond their wildest dreams, and they could lather all their other children with the wealth. You were nothing more to them than a ticket to prosperity and power. That's all. Your sacrifice bought them wealth, and through that wealth they would have earnt some sort of status in your village. If you leave here, you have no home. They'll never take you back. They *don't want* you back."

"No." I shake my head. His words send an icy cut straight through my heart and I turn, stumbling over the chair in my haste to get out of the room and back to my bedroom.

It's not true. My parents loved me. Everyone said my parents loved me, that they just showed that love differently, that I didn't understand how hard it was for them to raise me, knowing they were going to lose me.

But as Wulfrun's words echo in my brain, I realise he is right. I was never hugged the way my siblings were hugged. I never received gifts, or praise, or attention beyond that which kept me safe and undamaged.

I think back to the insistence I be kept 'pristine' for my werewolf captors. That's why I was kept safe. Because if anything happened to me, there would be no treasure, no payment. Certainly not for another twelve months when they would have to sacrifice Dasha, their beloved second-eldest daughter.

I throw myself on my bed, letting my tears fall, hating Wulfrun for his fucking truthfulness and honesty. As if he has any idea of my life, or what I've been through, or how my family feel about me.

Too soon there's a knock at my door and a chorus of apologies.

"Go away." I scream at the door, sliding off the bed to head to the shower, turning the water on full force. At least I can't hear them under the spray, and I sink to the floor, still fully dressed, and let the blast wash away my misery.

CHAPTER 9

I'd stay under the shower forever if I could, but all too soon all the hot water has gone, and now I'm not just crying, I'm shivering too.

I turn off the water, peeling off my wet clothes and leaving them in a heap on the shower floor. I dry myself off, and I'm wrapping myself in a thick warm dressing gown when I realise I can hear snarls and shouting, and thumps and bumps and bangs.

That's not my werewolves, is it?

I want to ignore it, but I've seen the effects of a werewolf fight, and as much as I hate them all right now, I really don't want any of them injured.

I open the door and creep down the hallway.

They're outside, all five of them. Ronther is leaning against a doorway, fresh blood visible through his bandages.

ONE GIRL FIVE HUNGRY BEASTS

The other four are in full battle mode, in werewolf form, three of them ganging up on the fourth.

I've only seen Ronther and Wulfrun in wolf form, so far, and only one wolf with the dark black fur that Wulfrun has. It's the only way I can tell that it's Wulfrun getting the beating of his life. There are deep scratches across his cheek and chest and back, kicks and punches and bites coming in from all angles.

I storm through the door, so angry that they can't even sort out their own issues like adults.

"What the fuck are you doing?"

They're so absorbed in their fight they don't even hear me above their snarling, continuing to beat and hit and lunge at each other.

"What are you doing?" I scream the words, certain the entire neighbourhood must be able to hear me, and still there is no response.

"You know those games you play with Merric?" Ronther hobbles forward, and puts an arm around my shoulder. I glare at him, why on earth is he going on about Merric's games now?

"Angry werewolf is a bit like berserker mode on those games. Their caught in such anger and fury that there's little that can pull them from it."

"Right," I say, through a clenched jaw. "So what will break them up?"

Before my eyes Ronther shifts into werewolf form. Shaggy grey fur sprouts from his skin, his nose lengthens into a snout, his ears shift location, sliding up either side of his skull until they're morphed into points on the top of his head. His whole body enlarges, stretching some of his bandages and tearing others.

It's terrifying to watch, and I take a step back, my heart racing. Is he going to rip me to shreds now? If nothing breaks through a werewolf's fury, how can they be conscious enough to make sure they're attacking the right person?

But Ronther doesn't attack me. Instead he lifts his head and lets out a long, low howl.

The fighting wolves stop as one, ears pricked, eyes on him. Once again Ronther begins to change, fur disappearing, nose and ears resuming their usual size and shape and location on his face. Stretched bandages fall to the ground, some of his wounds weeping afresh. He reaches out to grab the wall for support.

He nods at me. "There you go," he says through panted breaths.

"Thank you," I say, before turning my attention back to the others.

"What on earth is going on here?"

A wolf with grey eyes, that has to be Merric, steps forward, his eyes narrowed. "Wulfrun hurt you, so we are hurting him."

"What?"

"You heard Merric." A mostly pale grey wolf, with a dark streak along his spine and tail, speaks with Tormod's voice. "Wulfrun hurt you. You locked yourself in your room and were sobbing so hard we could hear you from the kitchen, and you wouldn't come out. We're just giving him what he deserves."

I shake my head, my hands clenched so tight my fingernails are stabbing into the palms of my hands.

"You all made me cry. All of you. With your stupid jealousies and assumptions. You all think you know everything." I glance at Wulfrun. "It just so happens that Wulfrun is right about most of the things he thinks he knows."

"Right. So he did make you cry." Thyrius pulls back a paw, claws extended, and I have to scream at him again.

"Stop! Just stop! I didn't cry because Wulfrun's words were horrid." I look at Wulfrun now, doubled over, blood streaking down his chest. "I cried because they were true, and I've known, for my whole entire life, and I didn't want to admit it."

There's an uncomfortable silence for a moment, and Thyrius lowers his arm.

"You think Wulfrun is right? That your parents didn't love you?" Merric asks the question. "What sort of parents wouldn't love their child?"

My eyes well up again and I blink, sending more tears sliding down my cheeks. "I always hoped I was wrong. I always tried to convince myself that the way my parents were over-protective of me was a sign that they really did love me, even though their every other action suggested otherwise. But I've never been loved, and I've never really been happy, and I realise now that this is not what fate has in store. I just have to do my duty and accept that this is the way my life is meant to be. I'm just not meant to be happy."

There's an uncomfortable silence, as all the werewolves relax their aggressive stances, and Wulfrun sinks to his knees.

Before my eyes they all change, shrinking into their human forms, what clothes have survived the change stretched and distorted and hanging loose on their bodies.

"Doing your duty doesn't mean you can't have happiness, too." Tormod steps forward with his arm out, but I take a step away from him. I don't want his comfort right now. "Perhaps you can still find happiness, in the life that you've been forced to live."

I shake my head. "I've had enough of all of you right now. I just want to be left alone for a while." I take a step towards the door, but then a thought crosses my mind and I glance back. "You guys had better look after Wulfrun." I look at him, doubled over in pain. "I've had enough of trying to help look after you all. There's too many of you, and only one of me, and the only time you seem to remember that is when you're complaining that you have to share."

I turn to Ronther. "You didn't fight again too, did you?"

He shakes his head. "I heard the commotion, and then the fighting, and I raced out here to see if I could stop it. I think I tore a few stitches in the process." He puts a hand on my shoulder. "I'm mostly

ONE GIRL FIVE HUNGRY BEASTS

healed, and these won't take too much longer. I'll be fine. You go and do whatever you need to do. Take time for you."

The kindness of his words sets my eyes watering again, and I wipe them with the back of my sleeve. I put a hand over his and give it a squeeze.

"Thank you, Ronther. You're the best." I don't mean for my words to cause any angst, but there's a new tension in the air, a new offense taken. I don't care anymore. Their reaction is their problem, not mine.

I turn to the others. "I'm going to bed. I've got to go back to Uni tomorrow, and I need my sleep. Just look after each other, please?"

There's a round of nods and muttered agreement, and I leave them to clean themselves up. I've had enough.

BUT IT SEEMS that just because I'm tired, doesn't mean I'm actually going to fall asleep.

I snuggle down under my blankets, and close my eyes, and then my mind replays the whole night all over again, the arguments, the crying, the fight. I wish I'd acknowledged my parents lack of feeling for me earlier. I can't believe I was so stupid as to hold on to it for such a long time, that even though I was forced to wait until everyone else had eaten before I could eat, that I received no birthday or celebratory gifts, that my every need over and above basic nutrition and shelter and safety was ignored, I still believed that my parents loved me. Even when they showered obvious affection on my sister and brothers. Even when, now I let myself admit it, they took away the only person who truly cared, by forcing him to be engaged to my sister. It made sense for Odran, it really did, better for him to give all his love to a girl who would be there for the rest of his life, rather than end up with a wife who would be taken before their lives had really begun. But every scrap of affection was taken from me, and now Wulfrun was right. I had no idea how to accept kindness and love from others. I was stuck, forced to spread myself thin so the werewolves could share a female partner. I toss and turn all night, finally dropping into a light sleep in the early hours of the morning, only to be woken a short time later by my alarm.

With such little sleep, I find it so hard to concentrate at Uni, and my puffy red eyes seem to announce to everyone what has happened.

"You had a fight with your men, huh?" An older woman, a couple of years above Dawn and I, takes a seat opposite us at lunch.

I shrug my shoulders, and direct all my focus on my food, wishing she'd go away. She doesn't seem to get the hint.

"That's good," she continues. I glance up at her in surprise.

"I mean, it's hard," she admits. "But it's still a good sign. Things are progressing."

I raise an eyebrow.

"What things are progressing?"

She smiles. "You can't form a relationship with someone, or several someones, until you've aired all the stuff that irritates you about each other. If you've done that then things should go a lot more smoothly for you from now on."

I shake my head. "They're so violent. They seem to think that the answer to any irritation is to beat each other up."

She holds my gaze. "Do they hit you?"

"No."

"Then don't worry." She shrugs. "They're bred to be violent—has anyone told you that yet? It's not ideal, but it's the way they are. It's encouraged from an early age. Helps decrease the population." She says it as though such a plan is perfectly fine and normal. "And don't forget that they need to sort through their irritations, too. It's not like they're best mates who happened to claim the same girl. They've been thrust into this just as much as you. Once they've sorted themselves out everything will go more smoothly between them, as well."

She reaches out to squeeze my hand. "I remember being new here, and all the feelings that go with that. But everything will be fine, I promise. You'll be so glad you were brought here, instead of being left with your village. Trust me."

She smiles, and leaves.

"Is she for real?" Dawn mutters, as we watch her go.

I think about my village and how unhappy I was there, how unwanted I felt.

"I think, maybe, she is," I say, realising that her words do feel right. And I think of Tormod's words the night before, that maybe we can make happiness out of the situation we're in, rather than expecting to get the things that we think might make us happy. My werewolf men have all gone out of their way to be nice to me and make me feel welcome in their own way. Perhaps it's time I return the favour.

"There's certainly a chance for more happiness here than I ever had in my village." I glance at Dawn. "And yours too, from what you've told me."

Dawn is quiet for a moment. "True."

In a way it's nice to hear from another woman who's been here for a few years, and at least have the hope of a brighter future, even if it's not guaranteed.

"I forgot the big news." Dawn interrupts my thoughts. "There was an announcement yesterday, when you weren't here. We have a huge exam in two weeks, to test us on what we've learnt so far in these introductory classes. If we pass, we get to move on to the next level, if we fail we have to start all these classes again from the beginning." Her shoulders are slouched, and I reach out to squeeze her hand.

"We can do this, Dawn. We've studied it enough and talked about it enough. Ronther is a great help to me with everything, I can help you with it too." I give her a smile, and her mouth lifts a little in the corners.

She takes a deep breath. "You're right. We *can* do this. Just have to think positive, hey?"

"Yes. And study." I roll my eyes and she laughs.

"Do you mind staying back for an hour or so every day after Uni, then, so we can go over everything and make sure we know what we're doing?"

"Not at all."

I WALK HOME, by myself this time, feeling lighter than I have since I first discovered I was destined to be a sacrifice for werewolves. I was a child then, my carefree life over in a moment.

But now, for the first time I realise that I do have some control over my life. I can study, get good grades, and maybe even find a job in this society, and some semblance of freedom to go along with it. I can at least form friendships with the men I've been forced to live with, find their good points and focus on those, instead of how unfair life is, and how I wish it could be different.

But when I get home the air is heavy. Ronther is napping in bed, though I can see he's removed some of his bandages, and there is no longer even the faintest sign of any of his wounds. Wulfrun is in the garden, heavily pruning a tree. He has a few bandages, but most of his wounds are open to the air. But those scratches I can see have healed remarkably well since the night before. I'd half expected Wulfrun would be bedridden for a few days, too. I'm glad to see that's not the case.

I'm about to go out when I notice that one of the branches he's cut had a bird from Tormod on it, and both bird and branch are laying on the ground, dented and damaged. Doesn't look like last night's outburst was enough to clear the air between him and Tormod, then.

Neither Tormod or Thyrius are anywhere to be seen, but Merric is in his usual spot, slumped on the couch, his thumbs moving fast on the video game controller as he hacks into his enemy.

"Mind if I join you?" I enter the room, and he looks up, his eyes wide.

"You want to play?"

"Sure, I think I'm starting to get the hang of it."

"Right. Yeah, sure. That would be great." He straightens up, passing me the spare controller, and getting out of the game so he can start one for two players.

"I didn't think you were interested. Wulfrun said video games bored you."

I shrug. "I couldn't play it all day, like you can. But now and again it's fun. It wasn't so much that the game bored me, I just felt so torn, with all the other things I thought I had to be doing. Actually it would be more fun if you would let me lead sometimes, and make decisions, not just give me instructions all the time. That's the bit that's boring, being told what to do with every decision. I'd like to make my own mind up, some of the time, just to see what happens."

"Ah, okay. I see. Sorry about that." He nods, and we enter the game.

This time, I stride ahead, my weapon at the ready, and take out the first two enemies we see.

"You are getting good at this." Merric offers me a smile. "Impressive."

"Thanks." I grin back, and settle back against the couch, eyes on the screen, ready for whatever might jump out at me next.

CHAPTER 10

*M*erric and I play for about half an hour, and working together as a team we get through so many different quests in the game's map, finding treasures and helping people and, of course, taking out plenty of monsters.

We've just defeated a boss, which I've learnt is the term for the bigger monsters, in a battle when I hear movement in the kitchen, drawers, not slammed exactly, but certainly closed with enough force to rattle the cutlery.

"That was amazing!" Merric says, lifting his hand for 'high five'. "I've never defeated that beast so quickly. We make a great team."

I grin. "We do. But I think I need to leave it there, for the moment." Merric's face drops but I reach out and give him a hug. "Play again tomorrow?"

He grins again. "It's a date."

I hand him my device and head on through to the kitchen. Wulfrun is slicing something with such speed I'm surprised he isn't cutting the tops of his fingers.

"Can I help?"

He glances up while his hand is still moving the knife, and I see, as though in slow motion, the knife catch the tip of his finger, and the wince on his face. Straight away the knife is dropped and he's wrapped his other hand around his finger.

"Ouch!"

"Shit. Sorry. I should've waited until you were done to interrupt."

He shakes his head, letting go of the finger, which has blood pooling on the top and then running down the side, to rummage around in one of the drawers. He pulls out a cloth which he wraps around the bleeding finger.

I head over and see a first aid kit in the drawer.

"Let me get that."

He steps aside, holding the cloth tightly around his finger tight while I try and find a bandage.

"That will do." He's nodding at the small sticky bandages on the top of the pile.

"What?" I pull out a small sticky bandage. "One of these?"

He nods. "It's only a small cut." He removes the towel to show me. There's a portion of skin distinctly separate from the rest of his finger.

"That's not small! It's deep. Shouldn't you go to the hospital, at least to get stitches or something?"

He shakes his head. "It'll heal overnight. Like these almost have." He indicates his bruises and cuts from the previous night. "Nothing to worry about."

Now that he's up close, I realise that all the other scratches and bruises he had after the fight the previous night are basically gone, it's just the fur that hasn't grown back that gives the illusion they're still there.

"It's a werewolf thing, isn't it? To heal quickly."

He nods and flashes a smile. "Saves a fortune on hospital bills."

I glance down at the chopping board, but it seems he moved fast enough that there's no blood on the board, or the food, thank goodness. A single drop has landed on the bench, but Wulfrun is already cleaning that up. I take the knife and find some detergent, giving the knife a thorough wash with some hot water.

"So, can I help you?"

"You want to help me?"

I shrug. "Sure, why not?"

"Because I made you cry."

I pass him the clean knife, and watch as he resumes his slicing, scraping the vegetable off into a pot of boiling water.

"Yeah, well. You were right. And it still hurts, but you guys have all been so good to me, I've got to return the favor. We can't really change our situation, can we? Better to make the best of it."

Wulfrun has one eyebrow raised, but he nods, even so. "You really want to make this work?"

I laugh. "It's not like I have any choice, is it?"

He tilts his head to the side. "Well, if things aren't working after one year, we can actually go our separate ways. I guess no one's shared that with you."

I shake my head. "No. I hadn't heard that."

"So that is something to think about. You don't actually need to force things with any of us, just because you think you have to."

I smile. "I won't force things, if *things* generally aren't working. But I won't know whether things are working or not unless I actually give it my best shot."

He returns my smile. "That sounds sensible."

He nods towards the lounge.

"You genuinely seemed to be enjoying your game in there tonight."

I smile. "I did. Because I explained to Merric that following him around was boring, and I needed to take part in the game, too. He listened and took that on. So we had a fun game."

"That's good. What about everyone else?"

"I haven't seen anyone else yet. Ronther was sleeping, so I didn't want to disturb him, and the others didn't seem to be home."

"No. They're out partying or something. That's Tormod's thing, you realise; socialising and partying." He watches me for a moment, before finally taking the next vegetable and beginning to peel it. "That doesn't really seem like the sort of thing you like to do."

"Let me do that." I reach out to take both vegetable and peeler from him. "I do prefer the quiet at home. But I've never really been to a party, nothing like what I've heard a party is, anyway, loud music, lots of people. My village had a limited number of people, and the music was never loud."

There's movement at the door and I turn to see Tormod and Thyrius standing there.

"Never had a party!" Tormod's mouth has dropped open in exaggerated horror. "We'll have to fix that."

My eyes widen, and I shake my head. "Not any time soon. I have an exam in a couple of weeks. I need to focus on that."

"An exam?" Tormod's eyes seem to light up. "We'll wait till you're done, and then have a party to celebrate!"

I open my mouth to object, but I can't. I just told Wulfrun I'd never had a party, and despite the thought of a house full of people making me want to hide away in my room, I'm desperate to do something for Tormod, the way I have for Merric and Wulfrun. I can't say no. I won't put a dampener on Tormod's enthusiasm.

Instead I force a smile. "That sounds great."

Tormod's grin grows wider. "Better get studying then! We want to make sure we're celebrating a success! You won't much feel in the mood for a party if you fail."

The thought of failure puts a dampener on things, though I keep my smile plastered to my face. Wulfrun gives my arm a squeeze, and offers me a smile of his own. He knows exactly how I feel about this, but for once he's not actually sharing. I smile back, genuinely, this time.

"Guess I'd better go see how Ronther's doing. See if he can help me out."

Thyrius follows me out into the hallway. "Before you do, I thought you might like this." He holds his hand out, another small beribboned box resting on his palm.

A gift, from Thyrius? Is he trying to compete with Tormod? He was so watchful of us in the garden the other day, when Tormod had me find the small creature. Did he imagine I enjoyed that? That that was a way to get to my heart? I take the box, my heart sinking, though I try to hide it. I'm not sure we can fit any more tiny creatures in the garden, and I really don't want to fill my room with them.

But when I undo the bow and lift the lid, it's not another creature that I find in the box. It's a small silver device, with a handle at one end.

"What is it?"

"Turn the handle and see." I glance up at him to see his eyes shining with excitement.

The device is so small I'm convinced I'll break it if I so much as touch it. I take the handle between my thumb and forefinger, and with the slightest amount of pressure, begin to turn the handle.

Instantly a sound emerges, a soft sweet sound that shocks me so much I let go.

"Keep going," Thyrius urges me on, and I turn the handle again. This time there's a sweet melody, and in an instant I'm transported back to my childhood, huddled in bed with my siblings, our mother leaning over us, singing this sweet lullaby. My eyes prick with tears at the memory.

"You know it?" He's gazing at me, directly into my eyes, and I nod.

"My mother used to sing that to me and my siblings when we were children, to help us sleep."

"Does it bring happy memories?"

I hesitate. Having just admitted to myself that none of my family really wanted me, it seems absurd to say this memory of my mother is happy, and yet it is.

I nod. "It's the only time I remember feeling safe, all snuggled up in bed with my brothers and sisters. She couldn't single any one of us out then. It was one of the few times I always felt included."

"I'm glad."

I shake my head. "How did you know?"

Thyrius shrugs. "It was a long shot, really. This belonged to my mother. The song is a lullaby her mother used to sing, though my father made the device. It was the only happy memory she had, too. She came from a village not too far from yours, so I hoped the tune was known throughout that area. I know it's hard, the move here, and everything that goes with it. I hope this will help you feel safe here, too."

Now my eyes are really welling with tears, and I have to brush them away.

"That's so sweet, Thyrius. Thank you. It's a perfect gift."

He gives a slight bow.

"I spent a lot of time considering what might suit you best. I wanted to make sure it was better than Tormod's, and I can see from your reaction that it is."

I sigh, and squash the disappointment. Doesn't he realise he's just ruined the moment? "It's not a competition, you know. Everyone is different. I'm sure you all have good and bad qualities."

He grins. "Yes. But some people's good qualities are better than other people's good qualities. Anyway, I'd better let you get back to see Ronther and get on with all this studying."

I nod. "Yes. And thank you, again."

I don't go straight to Ronther's room. Instead I head to my own, cradling the small musical box in my hands. It is perfect, and I push away the memory of Thyrius' competitive streak and choose to simply enjoy it for what it is. When the door is closed behind me I turn the handle again. I close my eyes as the music plays, letting the tears slip down my cheeks as I remember the huddle in bed, my mother's gentle voice, and that all-encompassing feeling of being loved.

IT TAKES me some time to compose myself. I wash my face and brush my hair, pulling it back into a low ponytail, before gathering up my books and heading up the hallway to Ronther's room. I realise as I get there that I probably should have checked first, but when I reach the door it's open, and when he sees it's me his whole face lights up.

"I wondered when I'd see you again."

I feel my face flush and I set my books down on the chair by his bed, sitting instead on the bed by his legs.

"Sorry about today. I should've come in this morning to see if you were okay."

Ronther shakes his head. "Don't be silly. You don't have to check on me. I'm well capable of looking after myself. I told you last night to take time for you, and I meant it." He reaches out to squeeze my shoulder, as I offer a grateful smile. "Now. I also just heard the conversation that Tormod is planning a celebratory party for you, just after your exams. So we'd better get to studying or else your party won't be any fun at all."

I pick up my books from the table.

"I won't find out the results straight away though, surely? Won't the lecturers have to mark our exams first? Can't the party simply be a celebration that the exams are over?"

Ronther shakes his head. "Your exams will be entirely on computers. They'll be mostly multiple-choice answers, and where they aren't, they'll be fed through to your lecturer as soon as you've written them. You'll know your results within half an hour of finishing."

Half an hour. I swallow the lump in my throat, but all it seems to do is add to the ball of fear in the pit of my stomach.

"So at Tormod's party I'll either be really celebrating, or I'll just want to escape everyone."

Ronther smiles. "You'll be celebrating. You know this stuff, Martha. The exam will be a breeze. But if I'm right, you'll just want to escape everyone, anyway."

I laugh, surprised at his insight, and give a small shrug. "Maybe."

CHAPTER 11

For two weeks I fall into a strict routine. University during the day, including a half hour study break afterwards with Dawn and some of the other women from our class, followed by a half hour gaming session with Merric, which Ronther says is important, because it gives my brain a chance to rest. Apparently a brain that is rested absorbs new information much easier than one that is not, and of course this has the much needed side effect of ensuring Merric doesn't get jealous about the amount of time I'm spending with Ronther. Actually, Ronther has thought of everyone. I have half an hour study time with Ronther before helping Wulfrun in the kitchen with dinner, then I spend most of dinner hearing Tormod rave about his party ideas, and then there's another hour study session after dinner, before going for a walk with both Thyrius and Tormod, which was also Ronther's idea, because he says exercise also helps pump oxygen around the brain, which means it is clearer and absorbs information much better.

The structure means that the two weeks leading up to my exam are so busy, and yet somehow they don't *feel* busy. What does happen though, is that the time flies by, and before I know it, I'm standing with Dawn and all my other classmates outside our exam room, butterflies jerking around in my stomach.

"I feel like I'm going to be sick." I close my eyes and take a deep breath, wishing I had something to still these nerves.

Dawn laughs. "You're just nervous," she says. "I'm told that's a good sign. Means you've studied, that you know your stuff." She glances around the room and I follow her gaze. Everyone else looks just as worried as we are, either pale and drawn, or fidgeting with their bags, or shifting their body weight from one foot to the other. When she looks back at me she forces a smile. "We've done our best, that's all we can ask of ourselves. Just remember to breath, and read the questions. That was Guthram's advice this morning, anyway."

Now it's my turn to laugh. "That does sound like good advice. Better than Ronther's anyway."

"Which was?"

"Don't worry about it, you know all this."

"Right. Well, it's nice to know he has confidence in you."

"That is true."

Before Dawn can say anything more the door opens and one of our lecturers stands in the opening.

"Each person is assigned a computer," she says. "Please find the one with your name on it. When the class is settled, the device will start up of its own accord. It's very simple, select your answer by touching the screen. There will be four questions that require thought out responses. When it is time to answer those questions, a sound proof booth will drop from the ceiling, and you can speak your answers into the microphone provided. Once the exam is finished, you may go to the courtyard. No one is to leave the building until every student has received her results."

I take another deep breath, blowing it out forcefully as students begin to file into the room. I really don't want to do this, and yet my feet follow Dawn's as she enters the room ahead of me.

Inside there are rows upon rows of tall metal screens, each with a seat in front of it. I scan the names, finally finding mine four or five rows in. As I sit down the device adjusts itself, the chair and screen moving to the best height, so that my feet rest on the ground, and the screen is at eye level. The movement makes the churning in my stomach worse, but I take a mouthful of water, the only thing we were allowed to bring in with us today, and feel ever so slightly better.

When everyone is seated, the lecturer announces that the exam goes for one hour, but we may leave as soon as we finish, if we get to the end earlier than that. Then it starts.

The hour flies by. As soon as the screen flickers on I give it my full attention, trying to remember to breathe, and to make sure to read the questions several times over, making sure I fully understand each one, before selecting an answer and moving on to the next one.

Out of the corner of my eye I catch sight of a soundproof pod emerging from the ceiling above a student nearby. I jump, as do most of those around me, convinced the ceiling is falling in before I remember what's happening. It moves silently from the ceiling, but it's not until a few have dropped that I get used to what they are and stop thinking the roof is about to collapse onto my head. It's a little distracting, but I seem to be flying through the questions and soon my own pod is lowering down around me. Instantly the room around me is silenced, and my ears feel like they're about to pop. A voice speaks the next question, which comes up on the screen at the same time, and I take a deep breath, recalling as much as I can about the topic so I can give as detailed an answer as possible. I lean forward, though I suspect I don't need to, to speak my answers into the microphone. Several times I have to cough to clear my throat, and my voice wavers, I'm so nervous, but soon I get through it.

When the pod lifts a single line flashes on the screen.

Thank you! My seat and screen move themselves to their original settings.

I glance around. There are a couple of other empty seats, though I see Dawn is still in her pod, her mouth moving as she answers the questions, though of course I can't hear what she is saying. I slide off the chair, and head to the door. The lecturer opens it for me, giving me a smile.

"Good luck," she whispers.

I nod. "Thank you!"

I'm not sure whether to feel relieved that I've finished so early, or fearful that I've gotten everything wrong. There's nothing I can do about it now, so I try to trust Ronther's certainty that I know my subjects and attempt to relax.

In the courtyard I grab a hot drink and find a spot to sit by myself. I'm not sure I'm ready for conversation yet.

When Dawn comes out she has a sort of dazed expression on her face, and I imagine I must've looked the same. She buys a coffee from the vending machine and heads over to sit by me.

"How did you do?" she asks.

I shrug. "I have no idea. It all went so fast. I think I did okay. I did remember to breath, *and* read the questions—" I give her a grin, and she smiles back, "—so hopefully that means I answered them correctly, too."

"Oh good! Me too." She takes a sip of her drink.

"My brain feels so... I don't know. On fire? Does that sound weird?"

I shake my head. "Nope. I'd say that pretty perfectly explains how my brain feels at the moment, too." I sigh. "I wonder how long the half an hour is? Does it start when we finish, or when everyone finishes?"

Dawn shrugs. "Your guess is as good as mine."

The courtyard is full of students by the time the lecturer emerges from the building. There's so much nervous chatter that it takes her a few minutes to get everyone's attention. When she does she brings up a list of names.

"These are the people who passed today's exam," she says. "Joanna, Ruby, Elizabeth, Greta—" Dawn reaches out to squeeze my hand as the lecturer continues to read out the names. I realise I'm holding my breath, but can't seem to let it go.

It takes a while to get through the list. Finally the lecturer reads the names we've been waiting for.

"Dawn, Martha."

We both squeal simultaneously, and start jumping up and down, wrapping our arms around each other.

The lecturer continues to speak. "Those of you whose names I did not read out, please come and arrange an appointment to speak with me in the next couple of days. You will be required to sit those classes again—"

I tune out, so excited to have passed, and look back at Dawn.

"We did it!" The grin on my face feels like it stretches from ear to ear, and Dawn's looks almost the same.

"We did! It's because you are such a great tutor, you know." She smiles at me.

I shake my head. "No. It's because we both put the work in and studied hard."

"Phew!"

"What happens now?"

Dawn smiled. "Guthram is taking me out to dinner."

I raise an eyebrow. "Guthram? Not any of the others?"

She shrugs. "Things aren't going so well with the others. I know we have to keep living together until a year is up, but I really don't see anything happening there."

"But Guthram?" From all that Dawn has said about Guthram, I guessed there was a spark of attraction there, and I'm so pleased things seem to be working out for Dawn and at least one of her partners. She needs something positive to look forward to, after her awful-sounding past.

A gentle smile breaks out across Dawn's face. "He's sweet. And he's gentle. He's more than happy to take things slowly and just remain friends, if that's how it turns out." She looks at me. "What about you?"

"Tormod is planning a party. Lots of alcohol, a few guests, loud music. I'm not actually looking forward to it, I doubt I'll enjoy it, but who knows. Maybe I'll surprise myself."

"Maybe." Dawn smiles. "Well, have fun."

"I'll try." I give her another hug and wave as she heads off. At least she's excited about her afternoon. I take a deep breath, and set off to catch the monorail. As much as I would love to take my time and walk home today, I think arriving late would probably be particularly impolite to Tormod.

AT HOME the music is already thumping. It's so loud I can hear it from outside, and I pause, wishing I could've spent the afternoon with Dawn instead. I wonder if they'd notice if I didn't turn up, but push that thought away. Tormod would notice.

I take a deep breath and go inside.

The walls seem to be vibrating from all the noise. I head into my bedroom to dump my bag. There's no escape from the music though, and I head off through the house, to see if I can find the source and turn it down.

Tormod is in the kitchen, filling the fridge with all sorts of bottles, and the benchtop is loaded with food. There are chips and dip and salads and carrot and cucumber sticks, and cake and biscuits and meat.

It looks like there's food enough for fifty people or more. My heart starts to race, and I take a deep breath in an attempt to slow it down.

"How many people have you invited?" I have to

shout, and even then I'm not sure Tormod actually hears me.

"Tormod!"

He turns. "You're home!" He's shouting too. "How did you go?"

"I passed." I call, and despite my irritation with all the noise I can't help but grin.

He gives me a hug, his voice down to normal level as he speaks into my ear. "Well done! I knew you would."

He pulls away, which means I have to shout again.

"Can we turn the music down? I can't hear you very well."

"What?" He puts a hand up to his ear, and leans in closer.

"Turn the music down."

He frowns. "Why? Don't you like it?"

I shake my head in exasperation. "I can't talk like this." My throat is getting sore already and I've only said a few things. "I just want to talk for a moment."

He gives me a thumbs up. "No worries! Why didn't you say so?"

He disappears into the lounge, and the volume drops by several decibels. It's such a relief. When he returns I ask again.

"So," I repeat. "How many people have you invited?"

He grins. "Only a handful." He gestures to the food. "That's Wulfrun's doing, not mine. He wants to make sure everyone has enough to eat. To be honest that should cover us for the party tonight, and feed the six of us for at least a fortnight!" He turns back to the fridge. "I'm in charge of the drinks. There's some soft drinks over on the sink." He waves in that general direction and I see half a dozen bottles of soft drinks. Nothing in comparison with the bottles he's loaded the fridge up with. "And I've sorted out all the alcohol. We've got beer, wine, mead, rum, vodka, whiskey—"

"Wow." I interrupt him, there are clearly a lot more bottles still to name. "Isn't that a lot for a few people?"

He shrugs. "I didn't know what you liked, so I got a bit of everything. This should last us a couple of parties, at least. Unless Merric drinks it all tonight, that is. He's started already." Tormod gestures to the lounge room, and I wander in to see Merric playing his game, half a dozen empty beer bottles by his feet, and another, half full, between his legs.

He's in the middle of a battle, but he glances up, his face lighting up when he sees me.

"You're home!"

He's looking at the screen again, his fingers moving fast as his character runs around the monster and attacks it from behind.

"How did you go?"

I take a seat next to him. "I passed."

"Fantastic! I knew you would."

In a few more moments he's defeated the beast, and he picks up his beer.

"You'll see Tormod is already in full party mode." He gestures to the kitchen with his beer, before taking a sip.

"So I see." I don't mention that Merric also seems to be in full party mode.

"You want a game?"

I shake my head. "Not this afternoon. I'm going to go and have a long hot shower, and then I guess I'd better prepare for this party. When is everyone coming?"

Merric glances at the clock on the screen. "You've got about an hour."

I nod. "Right."

I've never been to a party before, and I don't know what to wear, but when I get to my room I see someone has laid out a brand new dress across my bed. I lift it up by the hanger. It's so light, and such a beautiful shade of sky blue, and it shimmers as I move it.

"Surely this is a bit much for a house party?" I shake my head, and lay it back across the bed. Could I get away with wearing something else? Probably not. I wonder who bought it for me, but the answer doesn't take long to figure out. Who buys me the expensive presents? Thyrius. I feel a flash of irritation, and almost wish I hadn't asked him to stop singing to me. At least then he wouldn't be in direct competition with Tormod and his carved creatures. Still, at least Thyrius' gifts are useful, and it would be a lie to say that I didn't like either the dress or the music box. I can't say the same about Tormod's figurines.

I'M in the kitchen when people start arriving. It's mostly strangers, who greet me with a kiss on the cheek and a hug, and a brief congratulations once they've enquired about my exam results, and then disappear outside with a drink in their hand. The music volume seems to rise instantly, and I wonder how on earth anyone can hear themselves *think* with all the noise, let alone actually hold a conversation with someone else.

Merric stays in the lounge, so close to the speakers I'm surprised it's not damaging his hearing. He continues to play various different video games, and there's quite a crowd watching him, each person taking their turn to play and cheering each other on. As I watch, Merric drains his drink and looks around for another one.

"Any more beer?"

Several people glance around the room, and soon it's discovered there's no more alcohol, and someone volunteers to fetch more drinks. When they come back it's with an armload.

Wulfrun barely seems to leave the kitchen. He ferries food to a table outside, and another in the lounge, returning to make more sandwiches, more snacks.

"You need some help?" I ask, feeling really out of place amongst all these people I don't know.

He grins. "Nope. I've got it all under control."

"Are you sure? I could really use something to do right now."

He gives me a pointed look. "What you should be doing, is mingling. These are mostly Tormod's friends, but still, if this ends up being a long-term thing then you are going to meet them all eventually."

He has a point, but I'm not ready to do that just yet.

"Why so much food?"

"The more they eat, the less drunk they'll be. When Tormod came home with all that alcohol, I knew I had to feed everyone. The night would be over pretty quickly, otherwise."

I raise an eyebrow. "You want the night to last longer?"

He shrugs. "You need to really experience a party. This way there's more chance you'll agree to having one again."

"You like parties?" Wulfrun doesn't seem to be the type, and I can't help but see his obsession with the food as a different way to hide.

He grins. "I love cooking for parties. For people. There's something satisfying about feeding others."

The oven timer dings and Wulfrun looks up at me. "Go and enjoy, mingle. I'm sure you'll find someone you'll have something in common with."

I doubt that very much, but I head off to try. Outside it's a bustle of noise and movement, people chatting and dancing, one couple deep in the shadows, their tongues down each other's throats.

I see Thyrius and he raises his glass to me and heads over, his eyes travelling from my face to my feet and back again, clearly liking what he sees.

"You look beautiful."

My face flushes and I smile.

"Thank you." I look up at him. "I assume this is a gift from you?"

He grins. "Who else would buy you such perfect gifts?"

I laugh. That comment is definitely a well-covered jab at Tormod. "Who else indeed."

"It fits well then? I had to guess."

I nod. "You guessed well. It feels lovely."

He glances at my hands. "You don't have a drink?"

I shake my head. "Water will do for me, for now. I might have something later."

"Alcohol will help you enjoy the party more." He raises his glass as though showing me the sparkling golden drink in his cup might tempt me to have some.

I shake my head. "I'm sure it will. I just need to eat something first."

He points to the table. "Wulfrun's made plenty of food."

"Yes."

When I make no move Thyrius raises an eyebrow, but then someone comes over to talk to him, and I take the opportunity to slink away. In truth I'm so nervous about this party and all these strangers that I'm not sure I could actually eat anything. My stomach is churning so much I'm almost certain I'd bring it straight back up again.

CHAPTER 12

I glance around the back yard, wondering where Tormod is. Before I spot him a woman walks towards me, a huge round stomach preceding her as she crosses the yard.

"Hi, Martha?"

I nod.

"I'm Janelle. One of Tormod's friends."

I hold out my hand. "Nice to meet you."

"You too." She has long blonde hair, green eyes and a friendly smile.

"How do you know Tormod?"

"I met him at a nightclub once. It was the first one I'd been to, actually. One of my partner's, Jod, is his name—" she takes a moment to point out a man standing by the food table, "—he was keen for me to experience their music and dancing."

"I've never been. Tormod suggested it, but I'm not sure that's really my thing."

Her eyes widen. "You'd love it! It's just like this, only louder and more people. It's fantastic!"

I nod politely. *Definitely not my thing.*

"Oh!" She gasps and rubs her stomach.

"This is a really silly question, I know. But, I'm assuming you're pregnant?"

She flashes me another smile, her whole face lighting up. "I am. Six and a half months along. Little fella will be joining us soon."

She looks enormous for only being two thirds of the way through. "And this is your first?"

"No." She laughs, and I feel suddenly foolish. She doesn't look much older than me, surely it wasn't a silly question?

"Werewolf gestation is shorter than human gestation by a couple of months. This is my third pregnancy, but it's our fifth child. His first two lots of siblings were both twins."

I feel my eyes growing wide at the thought. Two lots of twins!

"Your babysitter must be busy then."

She laughs again. "I have five husbands, Martha. And only one who likes to party. The others are all at home, looking after their children."

Their children? I'm feeling more and more uncomfortable as the conversation progresses. "They don't mind looking after each other's children, then?"

Janelle looks confused. "They love their children. They're all so attentive to my needs and the needs of our children. Our family unit is solid, strong. Everyone is there to support everyone else achieving their life's dream." She glances at me. "You're still new here, and I know everything is so strange and new, and not at all like the way we do things in our home village. Because you're new I'll let you in on a secret. It's always best to have sex together. Every time. If everyone penetrates you, when you fall pregnant, the child or children belong to everyone. No if's, but's or maybe's. That's the way to do it."

There's movement across the yard, and someone is waving in our direction. Janelle notices and waves back.

"Oh, it's Hannah! I haven't seen her for ages. Was great to meet you." She gives me a smile, and I force one back as she disappears amongst the party goers.

I don't know what to make of her conversation. I don't want kids, and yet the idea of a big happy family where everyone supports each other and *loves* each other has just sent a pang through my heart.

I've always wanted to belong to a happy, loving family. To be one of the wanted, not the one always left out. I thought I'd missed out on that ever happening. It never occurred to me I could make it happen, with partners and children of my own.

I catch sight of Tormod, dancing with a group of other werewolves in the middle of the yard. He's clearly enjoying himself, but I'm so churned up I really don't want to join him there, so instead I venture back inside. I haven't seen Ronther yet, perhaps I can hide away with him.

As I expect, Ronther is working away in his room, headphones on, fingers moving across the keyboard so fast there's a constant tap of keys. I hover in the doorway. I really don't want to disturb him if he's busy, but he stops for a second, stretching his back and shoulders, and sees me.

"Come in," he says, sliding his headphones down to hang around his neck.

I close the door behind me and sit down on the spare seat he pulls across for me.

"What are you up to?"

"Escaping the party," he says with a grin, and I smile back. "Seriously though, I'm working on a program for the government. It's a way of identifying where each first-born human woman comes from and seeing how we can bring aspects from their home here, to make the transition easier for them."

"Wow. What does that involve? Do you go out to all the villages?"

"No." Ronther shakes his head. "That's someone else's job. I'm just trying to develop something that makes it easier to sort and store all that information and then retrieve it again. If we can get this up and running, we can set things in motion in the months before we collect someone, hopefully making the process a whole lot less stressful for everyone involved."

"So how does that work, the programming, I mean?"

Ronther's grin widens. "Well—" He starts to talk, and a string of words I have never heard before comes out his mouth and I find myself staring blankly at him.

"Sorry." I shake my head. "I have absolutely no idea what you mean by any of that."

He grins again. "That's okay. I can teach you, if you want."

"Maybe another time." I smile back. "But I am curious about compiling information on the villages. Who came up with that idea?"

Ronther shrugs. "I saw how much you were struggling. I didn't really know what I could do to help you, but I wanted to make it easier for the next person. So I put in a proposal to the government, and it was accepted, so I have a grant and the first teams are setting out soon."

I reach out to put a hand on his arm.

"You wanted to help me?"

"Of course. This situation we're in isn't really doing anyone any favours, but we can't do anything about it, except try and make it easier." He glances at me. "Not being able to develop a relationship with a woman before you're thrust together doesn't exactly help anyone get laid, and then having to share one woman with four other men just seems to exacerbate the problem."

I raise an eyebrow. "So, it's not completely selfless

then." I grin, moving my hand to rest on Ronther's thigh. "You just want to get into my pants."

He grins, and I see his pupils dilate before his gaze darts back to the computer screen. "Well, that would be the preferred outcome."

All of a sudden I feel such a rush of affection for Ronther. He helps me out every day with no pressure on me to give anything in return, and here he is, working, when he could be enjoying a party, so he can find a way to make this whole transition better for other women like me.

The thought of Janelle's happy family springs to mind, and suddenly my heart is shouting that that is exactly what I want. And I could have it, with Ronther, and Merric, and Wulfrun and Tormod and Thyrius. I lick my lips, suddenly aware of just how sweaty my hands are, and that I'm about to do something I swore I would never do.

I lean forward, and Ronther glances at me. His eyes widen in what looks like terror, quickly replaced by hope, and he shifts a little closer. I shouldn't be doing this. But suddenly I want nothing more than to experience Ronther's lips pressed against mine.

"Here you are!" The door swings open and Ronther and I pull away from each other as though we've been burnt.

"Wondered where you were hiding away." It's Tormod, his eyes a little unfocused, and slightly unsteady on his feet.

I'm blushing, but he doesn't seem to notice as he staggers towards us, a bottle in each hand. As he gets closer he holds one out to me. "Come on, have a drink. We're having so much fun out here."

I glance at Ronther who shrugs and gives me a sad smile. "You should probably go and enjoy this. It is in your honour, after all. It's okay. We can talk later."

I nod, as he puts his headphones on again, and I let Tormod put his arm around me and push me out the door.

"You've got to ignore Ronther," he says. "He hates parties. But don't feel bad for him. It's his choice to stay locked away. You should come out and have some fun!" Tormod's words are a little slurred.

"Should we get something to eat?"

My stomach isn't churning so much since sitting down with Ronther. Instead there's a sort of bubbly, excited feeling, and alongside it, a realisation that I haven't eaten since lunch time and I'm starving.

"Only if you have a drink first." He hands me the bottle, so I take it, twisting off the lid and taking a small sip.

"Wow, tasty." And it is. Very sweet and fruity, not at all like the mead Vallin makes in my village. One mouthful of that mead, and you know you're drinking alcohol.

"I knew you'd like it!" Tormod's grin grows, and he leads me outside, to the table loaded with Wulfrun's food.

He's a bit wobbly, and I feel like I'm propping him up as we walk, but when we get to the table he somehow manages to stand and dance around on the spot as I grab a plate and load it up with sandwiches and cold meat and salad.

"How are you going to eat all that?" Tormod frowns as he watches me pile food on my plate.

"I'm starving. I haven't eaten since lunch time. Can we go sit somewhere?"

"Alright." He leads me through the crowd, which seems to have thinned a bit since I was outside before, and we sit on the ground, the gnarled roots of one of the garden trees providing seating of sorts.

He watches me eat, reminding me every few bites that I have a drink I need to consume too.

"You're beautiful, you know that?" His voice is husky, and I find myself blushing, yet again.

"Even without Thyrius' expensive dress. Even when you're just in your casual clothes, or even that simple dress you wore from your village. My breath caught just looking at you. I was so glad when you picked me."

That's not exactly how I remember it, but I don't see the point in correcting him right at this moment. His eyes are ever so slightly unfocused as he looks at me, and there's a dreamy sort of smile on his face. "It's just a shame I have to share you."

How am I supposed to answer that? Right now I'm not even sure Tormod is aware of what he's saying, and I wonder if he would say as much if he were sober. Well, he probably would still wish he didn't have to share me. But how does he think I feel about the situation?

I finish my last bite of food and take another sip. A few people come over to say goodbye, and I realise that it must be getting late.

I shiver and rub my arms. "I'm feeling a bit cold. I might go inside."

Tormod nods. "I'll come with you."

We head inside, which is even emptier than outside. There are a couple of people gathered in the kitchen, chatting with Wulfrun. Merric is alone, still playing a video game, though the way he's slumped on the couch I wonder exactly how aware he is of what he's doing and how much is automatic. The room is littered with bottles and plates, and I wonder who, exactly, is expected to clean it all up in the morning?

Tormod leads me to sit down next to Merric, and then he sits on my other side.

"Finally got her to have a drink," he says to Merric, who holds up his own bottle to clink it against mine.

"Good to see. Got to let your hair down now and again." His words are a little slurred, too.

I sigh and take another drink. This is really sweet, and it goes down easily. When I finish the bottle Tormod hands me another one.

Merric has turned to me, one hand on my thigh the other resting along the back of the couch beside me. "You're pretty amazing, you know. I've been talking to other fellows, and none of the other gamers have a woman who will play games with them every afternoon." He burps, then laughs. "Shit, sorry about that." He brushes hair out of my face. "I just want to say that I really appreciate that about you. That you had a go, even when you weren't really interested. And I love it that you play with me. In fact, I just love you so much. All of you!" He glances up at Tormod. "Even the guys. You're all so amazing, such wonderful people, and I'm just so honoured that I got to meet you and be part of this amazing family." He shakes his head. "I just love you guys so much."

I turn away and take another mouthful of my drink. I can't sit here and listen to Merric, not when he's like this. It's just the drink talking, not him. As if he even *likes* the other guys! But Tormod is sitting beside me again, and I don't know how to move without seeming rude.

Tormod brings his mouth close to my ear, his warm breath sending a shiver down my spine. "Merric loves everyone when he's drunk," he whispers. "Even complete strangers."

I suppress a giggle.

"But if you leave now, he'll cry, literally. And then he'll be a sobbing mess for the rest of the night, which is really unpleasant to deal with, so can we just humour him until he falls asleep?"

I turn to glance at Tormod, and raise an eyebrow.

Merric is resting his head on the back of the couch, his eyes closed, a satisfied smile stretched across his face.

"Humour him?" I mutter. "How?"

Tormod shrugs. "If you drink more, he'll drink more, and maybe he'll fall asleep."

I take another mouthful, and then a few more. Soon I'm feeling quite buzzy, light-headed and happy, and it makes Merric's confessions of love much easier to bear.

"We love you, too," Tormod says, ruffling Merric's hair. "You and Ronther, you're the best, absorbed in your screens, quiet and out of the way. Gives the rest of us a better chance."

I find myself giggling, a high-pitched noise that I can't seem to stop. I don't know why Tormod's words are so funny, but they really are. I shake my head and blink a few times in a failed attempt to clear my thoughts, but the movement just makes the room spin so I stop, grabbing the arm of the chair instinctively to try to stop the spinning. It takes me a moment to realise the room is not spinning at all, and my grabbing the chair will do absolutely nothing.

"This drink is alcohol," I blurt out, holding it up to the light as though I'll somehow see the alcohol molecules better.

Tormod bursts out laughing. "Fairly certain you knew that when I gave it to you."

I frown. "Yes. I mean. It's really alcohol." I shake

my head and try again. "Really alcoholic! So potent! I've only had a couple."

Tormod nods. "Yep. It's good stuff."

Behind me Merric mumbles something and then begins to snore.

"There you go," Tormod whispers. "That didn't take long, did it?" He stands and holds a hand out to me. "Shall we go somewhere quieter?"

Anywhere away from Merric's snoring would be fine by me, and I reach up to take his hand, feeling unsteady on my feet as we shuffle towards the door.

"I think I need to lie down," I say, as the room continues to spin violently.

Tormod laughs again. "That's the plan."

But then Merric is awake again and up out of his chair, staggering towards us.

"Wait! I'm coming too."

I giggle again, stumbling against Tormod as he tries to hurry us out the door, Merric stumbling behind. We get to my bedroom, and Tormod pulls off my dress, and helps me into bed. I'm ever so grateful, until he climbs in next to me.

"What are you doing?"

"I just want a kiss."

I laugh. A voice in my head says no, but there's another voice asking, 'What would a kiss hurt?' A kiss might be nice, actually. I think about the imagine in my head of Janelle's family, five husbands, and five babies, all playing happily together, everyone loved.

I tilt my head up, closing my eyes as Tormod's

lips press against mine. His lips are soft, but his breath reeks of alcohol, and I end up coughing.

He doesn't seem to mind, moving to kiss along my jaw and nuzzle at my neck. It tickles a bit, and I laugh, but I'm also feeling so tired.

"I just need to lay down," I repeat. Tormod lowers me onto the pillow and lays down next to me.

"Do you want to take it further?" he asks.

"Further?" I'm not sure what he means. "I'm just tired," I say, rolling over to snuggle down into my blankets.

I WAKE up with a pounding head and a dry mouth. I open my eyes, but the light is too bright, and I have to clamp them shut again. I try to bring my right arm up to rub my temples, but it's stuck, and I realise I can't remember a whole lot from last night.

Wulfrun made heaps of food, Tormod had lots to drink. I remember the conversation with Janelle, about her family. I remember sitting with Ronther, almost kissing him, and there's a warmth that spreads through my chest at the memory.

Then Tormod came, and we sat with Merric and drank for a while, and then—

There's a snore to my side, right where the strange weight is on my right arm, and my eyes fly open. Merric is there, wearing only a pair of trousers, one arm flung out to hang over the side of my bed, his head thrown backwards.

"Ah!" I squeal as I pull my arm out from under him and sit up, only to realise there's someone else in the bed, too. Tormod! And I'm wearing only a bra and underpants, my beautiful blue dress thrown over the chair beside my bed.

I begin to slide backwards off the bed, taking handfuls of blankets and pulling myself towards the end of the bed.

Tormod opens his eyes, his grin stretching across his face as he looks at me.

"Good morning, beautiful."

I scream again, only to have the door behind me open and Thyrius, Wulfrun and Ronther burst in.

"What's happening, is everything okay?" Wulfrun's eyes are wide, but then he looks at me, and them, and a slow grin crosses his face.

"Did you—"

I raise a hand, holding it out, palm flat, towards him.

"Stop."

He stops.

"I don't know." I rub my forehead. "I can't remember."

Merric blinks sleepily, his eyes opening wide when he sees us all gathered together and my state of undress.

"Woah. Did we—"

I shake my head. "I don't know," I repeat. "I don't know what happened."

Tormod begins to laugh, and I glare at him. "I'm glad someone is entertained by all this."

"Nothing happened," he explains, through his laughter. "We kissed, and then I lay you on the bed and started kissing your shoulder, and then you started snoring! And then Merric came in and lay down next to you and fell asleep as soon as his head hit the pillow."

I raise a brow. "And you stayed?"

He shrugs again. "I was tired. Besides, I didn't want Merric waking up and trying his luck with you. I had to stay to protect you."

"Right. Because you weren't trying your luck before we all fell asleep."

"Hey." He looks at me. "You were enjoying yourself. You didn't hold back."

I feel my face flush, and I climb off the bed.

"I need to shower. You can *all* leave my room now." I glance at the three men by the door. "Clearly I'm fine, and nothing happened, so no one needs to be worried about anything."

Wulfrun is smirking at me, and I know he can see how much it's frazzled me. I truly can't remember. I have to trust that Tormod is telling the truth, and I don't know if I can.

I stand with my arms crossed, waiting for them to leave. Wulfrun stays by the door until everyone has left, then he smiles at me. "He's telling the truth, just so you know. If Tormod had actually slept with you, he wouldn't be able to keep it to himself. We'd all know."

He follows the others out, closing the door behind him, and I sink to the ground, my head in my hands, so relieved that I didn't just have sex for the first time, when I was so drunk I couldn't remember it.

That would be the worst.

CHAPTER 13

It's a week before I'm back at Uni and can continue with some sort of routine. There are new classes, and a few new faces, women who failed the exam for this second lot of classes and have had to stay back.

Dawn tells me about her date with Guthram, and I try to listen, smiling and nodding in what I hope are appropriate places so she doesn't feel ignored, but what happened at the party just plays over and over in my mind. I almost kissed Ronther, by choice, without any alcohol involved. I wanted to kiss Ronther, and if I'm honest with myself, I still want to kiss Ronther. I dismiss that thought.

I want the happy family Janelle spoke of, which seemed so realistic amid all the noise and hustle and bustle of the party. But it's daylight now, and I know too well that not every family ends up happy, and that just because one woman has the perfect life doesn't mean that will happen for everyone. *And maybe her life isn't as perfect as she made it sound.* Once the thought is there I can't get rid of it. Because it's true after all. No one's life is perfect.

But it was that hope that led to what *almost* happened with Tormod, and possibly Merric. Well, not just that hope. It was definitely encouraged by the alcohol. And possibly some underlying attraction, too. Not that I want to admit that out loud. They are both thoughtful and sweet, in their own way, Tormod with his carved animals, Merric with the games he just wants to share with me. If I'd not had those drinks, would I have ended up passed out in bed with them? I'd like to think that I would have ended up in my bed alone, but there is a little part of me whispering in my ear that I really did want things to go further, despite what I tell myself.

In that case, if I hadn't been drinking, would I have ended up having sex with Tormod, and possibly Merric as well?

My face burns at the thought, and my rational brain says there is no way I can let that happen. But my body is telling me something completely different. There's a shiver travelling my spine, at the thought of having sex with any of the men, and my nipples are tingling, and oh god I don't want to admit it, but there's a warmth spreading out from my groin, and a dampness between my legs. Fuck.

I know I can't face any of them. My face burns

the moment any of them try to speak to me and I spent the two days after the party hiding away in my room, complaining of a hangover, but I also know I have to face them, eventually.

When I get home that afternoon Thyrius is waiting on the doorstep for me.

"I bought you this," he says, handing me a long, thin package. When I open it it's an eye mask. "It's for the next hangover. Thought it might help you get over it sooner."

There's a smirk on his face, and I take it without a giving him so much as a thank you, and push past him into the house. I see Wulfrun coming down the hall, and I duck into Ronther's room before he can speak.

Ronther looks up in surprise.

"I just wondered if you could help me study?" I say, stuttering over my words.

"Of course."

He sets aside whatever it is he's doing and I move to sit next to him at his desk.

"Why don't you read out what you've done today."

I nod, and open one of my books. I start to read, but Ronther isn't looking at the page, as he usually does. Instead he's gazing at me. I glance up, and he gives me a hopeful smile. I force a smile in return and go back to my reading, but out of the corner of my eye I see he's still gazing at me.

Before too long there's a knock at the door.

"Just me," Merric calls. "Wulfrun thought he saw Martha come in here. Just wondered if she wants a game?"

Ronther is still watching me. I can tell he's hoping for a kiss, but I just can't allow that to happen. I stand abruptly. "I'm finding it really hard to concentrate today. Perhaps it's because I forgot to give my brain some time."

Ronther nods, and I close the book and scurry from the room. At least with Merric I know his attention will be on the screen.

But Merric's attention is just as lost as everyone else's. He keeps glancing at me out of the corner of his eye, spreading his legs wide so one leg rubs up against mine. At one point he complains his arm is sore from holding the controller up for so long, and he rests his arm along the back of the couch, just behind my shoulders.

I ignore it, giving my character on the screen my full attention, blasting through the obstacles all on my own, Merric's character trailing behind. On any other day there'd be a feeling of smug satisfaction from leaving Merric behind, but today all I can think about is the intensity of his gaze.

Tormod arrives home, entering the lounge room and grinning down at me in a way that just makes me shiver, and I'm on the verge of pushing past him to go hide in my room when Wulfrun announces dinner is ready.

In the dining room I keep my eyes on my food,

responding to questions about my day in as few words as possible.

I can't look at any of these men or Wulfrun will know exactly how I'm feeling. He probably knows exactly how I'm feeling anyway.

When he finishes, he stands to take my plate, our fingers brushing as he picks it up. I snatch my hand back, mutter something about being tired and scurry to my room.

The next day is even worse. Dawn informs me she's had sex with Guthram, and it was the most amazing experience of her life. She says that some of the other men have been really nice too. She's kissed them, and said that maybe having five husbands is actually not such a bad thing.

I can't understand how she's changed so suddenly, and wonder what sort of miracle worker Guthram is that he's managed to woo her into bed with him!

I'm fighting with myself, arguing that life would be much better if I just never said yes to any of these men. There's too many of them, and they're too jealous of each other. If I let myself fall any further, I'm bound to get my heart broken, and one or more of them is likely to be beaten to a pulp

And yet... what about Ronther's lips? What would they feel like against mine? Or Merric's hands on my breasts? Or Wulfrun's—I shake my head.

Woah. Don't go there! I can't let my thoughts wander anymore. It's too dangerous.

When I get home this time, the house is empty of everyone except Thyrius, who is waiting in the kitchen for me with a glass of water.

"I'm not sure I've ever been home when Wulfrun isn't here." I force a laugh to cover my nerves.

Thyrius laughs, too. "Yes, Wulfrun tries to make sure he's home when you are. But it seems there are road works between here and the market, and he's currently trapped in traffic. Could be some time."

I look at Thyrius. "You sound like you planned it."

He shrugs. "The road has needed improving for months. Everyone knows that. I may have just paid someone to work at this particular time." He grins, and I'm not sure whether to believe him or not. And if I do believe him, should I feel threatened by him, or relieved he got me some time at home without Wulfrun's ever watchful presence? "It's so hard to get a moment alone with you, Martha." Thyrius takes a step closer. "You're always busy at Uni, or studying, or giving your brain a rest on that silly video game of Merric's." There's a slow smile that spreads across his face, and I lick my lips, my stomach a bundle of nerves. He's so close to me right now. Is he going to kiss me? If he does am I going to kiss him back? I really just want to say no and go hide in my bedroom, but something has glued my feet to the floor and I can't tear my eyes from his face.

"I bought you something." He holds out another small box, and I reach out to take it, desperate for the distraction. Inside there's a necklace with a single tear-drop crystal pendant.

"Can I put it on?" His voice is low, and husky, and it does things to my body I swore I wouldn't allow.

I swallow, and nod, reaching to lift my hair up out of the way.

He's so close now, as he reaches around my neck to do the clasp. He's wearing a new aftershave, I realise, something spicy, and I breathe in deeply.

"You like?" His mouth is so close to mine. I nod again, and then his mouth is *on* mine, his lips so soft. I close my eyes, reaching my hands out to rest on his firm chest. His tongue slips between my lips, seeking out mine. He tastes so nice, like cinnamon and nutmeg and stewed apples. I never would have imagined he could ever taste so good.

There's noise as the front door opens and, Wulfrun enters the house, a jumble of bags and curses.

I pull away, but Thyrius reaches out to pull me in for one more kiss before letting me go. "Guess I should give him a hand," he says, winking at me.

I nod, and Thyrius leaves the room, leaving me feeling dazed. I close my eyes, then realise with a start that Wulfrun is heading here.

I take a huge drink of the water Thyrius has left, drinking so fast it overflows and spills down my chin. As I lower the glass Wulfrun reaches the door, and our eyes meet. I can't imagine what he sees, but I know my face is flushed, and my lips must be swollen.

He scowls, and I can see in an instant that he knows something has happened. Even if he doesn't know what.

I nod a hello and flee to the safety of my room.

I ALMOST CAN'T BEAR to attend university, with Dawn glowing from the apparently amazing sex she's having, and when the lecturer announces that instead of our normal class we will be having a lesson on basic sex education, a large part of me wants to run away.

I don't. I'm sure my absence would be noted, if not by the lecturer, then certainly by Dawn. Then I'd have to get the run down from her, and I'm not sure I'm ready for more of those types of conversations.

But that isn't the only reason I don't skip class. There is another part of me that is curious. How different are these men from 'normal' human men? Not that I've seen a 'normal' human naked to be able to compare the two. But still. *If* I give in to my body's urges, and my heart's hope, then I really do need to have some idea of what I'm doing.

Dawn grins at me.

"This might help you," she whispers, when the lecturer turns back to the screen at the front of the room.

I frown. "What do you mean?"

She raises an eyebrow. "It's clear you've been conflicted about something this whole week. I know you didn't want to have sex with any of your men when you first came here, but you're allowed to change your mind. It's okay to change your mind. No one will think any different of you."

I shake my head, but the lecturer is facing the students again.

What Dawn thinks of me isn't holding me back. It's this whole bizarre situation we're in. If I had not been the first daughter, then I probably would have been married to Odran right now, possibly even pregnant with our first child. I imagine I would be fearful of the birth, of whether it was going to be a daughter who was taken away, or a son we could keep. And until I'd had one daughter, I'd be fearful of that with every pregnancy. It didn't matter if it was the eighth child who was a girl, if she was the first born to the family, she'd be gone.

But now I'm in a situation where any child I have is mine to keep, and judging from the way the werewolves treat women, she'll probably be loved and showered with affection her whole life, treasured, as I never was.

It occurs to me that I never wanted children because I never wanted to be forced to give one away. But now I don't have to. I can succumb to romance, and sex, and children, without that fear looming over me.

It's like a weight has been lifted from my shoulders. But can I trust it? I turn my attention back to the lecturer.

"It's so, so important," she says. "That you know

your own body, and what it is that feels nice to you. I can tell that some of you have already passed this point—" There's a giggling among some of the students at the front of the room. "—But for those who haven't, it's really important that you take the time to explore your body. Use your fingers to apply different pressure at different locations. Sometimes the softest touch can be enough to turn your libido sky high, sometimes you want something firmer. Fast and slow movements can also cause different reactions, and don't forget pinching and squeezing certain spots, like your nipples for example, can really help you get hot and juicy for your men."

Just the talk is enough to get me squirming in my seat. When she brings up a picture of male anatomy, and begins to point out particularly sensitive spots, I feel myself getting wet there and then.

"Well, I have to admit I missed the self-pleasuring part," Dawn murmurs to me as the class finishes. "But Guthram was pretty good at helping me in that regard. And everything else is pretty accurate."

I find myself blushing and wishing I was able to drain the blood from my face every time it happened.

"Hey, don't worry about it." Dawn nudges my arm. "It'll happen when it happens. But I'm sure it can't be too far away for you."

I shake my head. "I told you I don't want children. I never intend to consent to sex." The words sound hollow, even to me. My brain might insist that celibacy is still the plan, but I'm not sure it's strong enough to control the desires running through my body.

"Yes. You did. But that doesn't mean that you still feel that way." She smiles at me, and it's friendly, not a smirk, but I can't help but wonder how she can read my very thoughts.

"I can see it in your face," she says. "You're curious, and that's the first step." We walk out of the building and see a vehicle parked nearby.

"There's Guthram. We're going to experiment with some of the other men tonight. Wish me luck!" She waves and is gone before I can say another word. Not that I can think of anything to say. Does she have to tell the world? Shouldn't that sort of thing be private?

I feel my face flush again. I'm being so ridiculous. We all have five partners, every single woman in this city. Even if we don't have sex with all five, it's highly likely we'll be sleeping with more than one. I just need to get over myself.

I walk home today. I need some space to think about all these feelings I'm having.

I wonder about my men. Thyrius, Ronther, Merric, Tormod, Wulfrun. What would it be like with each of them? What would it be like with all of them? Ronther is so gentle and shy. I can't imagine he would be any different in bed. And Merric is so laid back, though there is an almost aggressive feel about the way he's been hitting on me lately. And Wulfrun.

Wulfrun knows everything, almost before I know it. Would he be a gentle lover? Thoughtful? I'm feeling wet again, thinking about them all, or more specifically thinking about sex. What about more than one? Would they all want to have sex at the same time?

That thought terrifies me, and I push it away. How on earth would any woman manage five men at once? It's got to be impossible.

CHAPTER 14

I've been deep in thought for the whole walk home, and all of a sudden I'm here, already.

Inside, Wulfrun is standing in the kitchen door. One look at him and I feel such a strong sense of desire it scares me, and I flee to my bedroom.

He'll know. If I look him in the eye, he'll know what I'm feeling, and how will I say 'no' to someone who can see that I really want to say 'yes'?

I pace the room. I'm so full of nervous energy, I don't know what to do with it all.

My nipples are tingling, my cleft is tingling. For the first time in my life I want to be touched, I want to experience what it is to have someone touch me, and kiss me, and fuck me.

I throw myself down on the bed, one hand sliding down my trousers while the other squeezes a breast.

Our lecturer said that exploring ourselves was a

great way to learn what works, and also a good way to let off steam. Perhaps that's what my body needs. Perhaps I can get myself off, without having to resort to any of the men. My fingers run through my pubic hair and part the lips of my vulva. Inside is so wet and slippery, and I've barely even started touching myself yet. Could it be all this talk? I never thought words alone could turn a person on, but then I'm having all these thoughts – the naked image from our sex education class today, with Wulfrun's head.

I push it aside. I can't think of Wulfrun. He'll know the moment he looks at me.

I think of Ronther instead. Ronther, who's there for me whenever I need it. Who never forces anything on me. I find my clitoris and begin to rub it. But then Ronther's face is replaced by Merric's, who's replaced by Thyrius, and then Tormod, and though I'm squeezing my breasts and rubbing my clit something just doesn't feel right. I'm feeling pleasure, but there's something missing too, and I groan in frustration. It's just making me want them all the more. I need to find someone to help me, but who? Which one would be best?

I head for the shower first, turning the cold tap on full blast and standing under it for as long as I can bear it.

It works, marginally. I dress, and take a deep breath, and steel myself for facing my men.

Wulfrun is still standing in the doorway to the kitchen, or perhaps it's just coincidence that I've caught him in the same spot. He says hello, but I duck my head, murmuring a 'hi' as I duck into the lounge room. I just can't face Wulfrun yet. Merric is the safest choice. We can play his game and just focus on the screen and not each other, but when I go in the lounge Ronther is there too, reclining in one of the armchairs, reading a book.

"The house is quiet," I say, sitting down next to Merric. "Where is everyone?"

Merric shrugs. "Thyrius has some inheritance row with his brother, so he's off dealing with that, and Tormod has gone to a party at the University." He glances at me. "He left earlier. I think he was hoping to catch you after your class - before you left the uni, to see if you wanted to go."

I shake my head. "I didn't see him anywhere. Must've missed me."

Inside I'm breathing a sigh of relief I didn't get dragged along to a party today. I don't think adding alcohol to my mixed-up hormones is a really good idea, considering how confused I'm feeling right about now.

Merric reaches down and I realise he has several empty beer bottles at his feet and a couple of full ones ready to go.

He twists the top, giving the beer inside a moment to fizz and then settle, before taking the lid off completely and taking several mouthfuls.

"There's something different about you today,"

Merric says, glancing my way briefly before returning his attention to the screen.

"Different?" I frown and stare at the screen, pretending to be interested in what he's doing.

"Yeah. You're all jittery."

"No, I'm not."

Wulfrun appears at the door, the movement causing me to glance up, a jolt of fear travelling my body before I manage to just as quickly look away.

I pick up the spare controller.

"Can I have a go?"

"Sure." Merric takes another mouthful of beer before flicking through the settings to add me as a player.

"I was just about to say dinner is ready," Wulfrun speaks up.

"I'm not hungry right now." I give all of my attention to the game. "Perhaps you could put it in the fridge, and I'll warm it up later."

Merric grins. "You heard her – we've more important things to do right now than eat."

Merric takes another swig of beer, offering me the bottle. I'm so tempted to take it, but I can't lose control. I shake my head.

He shrugs. "Plenty there if you want some. Just help yourself."

I ignore him, and Ronther too when he gets up to go and join Wulfrun in the dining room. I feel a twinge of guilt. Neither of them deserve to be ignored, but I'm so scared of opening up to them that the guilt is not enough to make me do anything about it.

Merric and I play on, as he adds to the empty bottles on the floor and then eventually Ronther returns, taking his place in the chair and picking up his book. I can hear Wulfrun in the kitchen, washing the dishes and tidying up. There's banging and clanging, as drawers and cupboards are slammed shut, and pots and pans are put away.

"He sounds cranky," Merric observes.

"Just a bit frustrated, I think." Ronther glances as me before returning his gaze to his book. I feel my face flush again and set the game controller down on the couch.

"I think I need an early night."

I stand to walk across the room, but then Ronther talks to me.

"How was Uni today?"

His question brings to mind the full frontal of a man's anatomy, and the lecturer's talk on self-pleasure, and I'm wet in an instant.

"Good." I try for a non-committal answer, but my voice seems to break and the word comes out as a squeak.

"Sex ed day today, if gossip on the street is right?" Merric smirks.

I spin around. "How did you know?"

Merric shrugs. "Like I said, word on the street. Everyone's talking about it. It's why there's a party at the Uni. The class always makes all the women wet, and most of them are ready to have a go, if they haven't already." He winks at me, and now my face is burning.

"Yeah, well."

I turn to leave, but Merric stands, reaching out to grab an arm and spin me back around to face him.

"You're horny, Martha." His voice is low and husky. "We don't have to be Wulfrun to know, we can all see it. Why not just give in to what your body so clearly desires?"

He cups my chin, and before I know it his lips are on mine and a zap has travelled my spine and I'm kissing him back.

I'm not ready. The fear is so strong that I push him away and flee back to the safety of my bedroom.

Inside I lock the door and lean against it, my eyes closed, trying desperately to catch my breath.

I want him. I groan inwardly and slide down the door, resting my head in my hands and my elbows on my knees. I really want Merric. And Ronther, and Thyrius and Tormod, and most especially Wulfrun.

How? How could this happen so fast? How could five complete strangers become so attractive to me, so quickly? They're werewolves, for goodness sake. They can turn into vicious animals at the slightest provocation. I've seen the process, and it's not pretty. They fight among themselves, constantly. I can't let this happen. I can't let myself fall for them.

"Are you okay?"

Wulfrun's voice jerks me back to the present, and I jerk to my feet, my mouth agape.

"What are you doing here?"

"I'm sorry. I just… we have to talk, and you've been avoiding me, so I came here to talk."

I shake my head. "We can't talk here, or now. It's not a good time. You have to go."

He runs a hand through his hair.

"I'm not leaving until I've said my piece. I'm sorry for the way I spoke about your parents. I thought you'd forgiven me, that we were moving past that, but you're avoiding me, and I think I know why."

He's looking at me, and I think… surely not? But I *think* that he has tears in the corners of his eyes?

"You were right when you said that I always make assumptions about people. I always know when things are right or wrong, I can pick up when people are telling the truth. Except with you."

He's holding my gaze, and I feel a shiver travel my spine at the intensity of it.

"I thought we were getting on. I thought, well, you heard what Merric said, about your class today, and how that affects people. It's common knowledge, locker talk among the werewolves, I guess. I was arrogant enough to assume you'd come home and want to have sex with the first person you saw, and I wanted that person to be me. So, I stood in the kitchen doorway. But when you saw me you ran into your room. And then you wouldn't speak to me when you finally came out, and for the first time ever you turned down dinner."

Oh god. If he only knew. I want to say something, to tell him he's right, that I really did want to jump him the moment I saw him, but I can't. I just can't let it happen, even though I desperately want to. Even though watching him, hearing him talk like this is making me burn up inside.

He shakes his head, and begins to pace the room. "I know I am abrupt at times. And far too open about the things I pick up, and I know that can make people uncomfortable. I thought you were different, I thought I could be that way with you, that you liked that about me, but it seems I was wrong. So I want to apologise if I've made you uncomfortable, and let you know that I will leave you alone from now on. I'll stay, and keep cooking you dinner until the year is up, and then I'll leave you and everyone else here in peace."

"I—" I don't know what to say. I can't tell him he's right. I *want* to tell him he's right. My brain is screaming at me that this is an easy way to remove one man from the equation, but my body has taken over and it's refusing to let such blatant lies pass my lips. What would be the point anyway? This is Wulfrun. He'll know whether I'm telling the truth or not.

His eyes meet mine, and I lick my lips. I realise my breath is shallow and fast, and I take a deep breath to try and even it out.

Almost instantly Wulfrun's eyes light up.

"Unless I misunderstood the reason you were avoiding me?"

He takes a step towards me, and it's all I can do not to throw myself at him.

"I—" I want to tell him it's not what he said about my parents, and it's not his over-the-top insistence on honesty and truthfulness, and yes, I am avoiding him for other reasons, but before I can get any of that out he's right in front of me and my heart is pounding, and I can't tear my gaze from his.

"I've been right in my reading of you, haven't I?" He reaches out to put a hand on my shoulder, one finger trailing down my bare arm.

I close my eyes. I had doubted the lecturer when she said the faintest touch could turn a person on better than anything, but it's happening to me right here, right now.

When Wulfrun speaks again his voice is husky.

"You want this as much as I do, don't you?"

I open my eyes, and he's as close as he can possibly be without touching. I can smell his aftershave, musky and masculine. I can feel his body heat, so close to mine. I just want to feel his lips on mine, and he knows it just as much as I do.

I tilt my chin up. Wulfrun needs no further encouragement. His lips are on mine in an instant, both hands on me now, strong and warm on my shoulders.

His tongue pushes between my lips. He tastes of spice and heat, the curry that is his favourite meal to cook. I wrestle his tongue with my own as I push my groin against his leg, my hands holding either side of his face as we explore each other's mouths.

He begins to grind against me, and I can feel the bulge in his trousers. My hands wander down to find the button and unzip his fly. I slide a hand inside to cup his cock.

He groans into my mouth, grinding against my hand.

"You have no idea how long I've been waiting for you to do that!"

He lifts me, so fast I'm barely aware that I'm moving before I find myself on my back, on my bed. He's pulling at my clothes, and then I'm naked and he's on all fours over the top of me, kissing me again.

I reach down to free his cock from his underpants, marvelling at how smooth the skin is around such a thick hard shaft, but then he breaks away, leaving me gasping for breath.

He kisses down my neck, all the way down my body until he is between my legs. I have no idea what he could possibly be doing, and he seems to know that because he gives me such a wicked wolfish grin, holding my gaze as he stretches out his tongue and flicks my clitoris with it.

My whole body jolts as though I've been zapped by lightning. He grins again, this time running his tongue ever so gently along my vulva, and this time I'm gasping.

My nipples are tingling, desperate to be touched,

and with Wulfrun's attention focused elsewhere I take a breast in each hand, rolling and squeezing my nipples between my fingers. The action sends tingles down my spine to add to the waves of pleasure emanating from between my legs as Wulfrun circles my clit with his tongue, sucking and flicking and sending me wild.

Soon my hips are thrusting, completely on their own, as his tongue delves deep inside me. It feels so good and I'm gasping, holding back moans that I'm sure would alert the whole house to what we are up to.

I feel the pleasure spiralling upwards, and finally I can't hold it in anymore and I throw my head back, a long low moan escaping my lips.

"Fuuuck!"

Wulfrun sits up, his grin wide.

"You seemed to enjoy that."

I'm too exhausted to speak. It was incredible, but how do I put that in words? Instead I reach down to run my fingers through his hair, lose and messy now, and pull him towards me, arching my neck so I can kiss him, long and deep.

He slides up my body, and I feel his cock, rock-hard against my leg. I reach down to wrap my hand around it again, but he presses my legs apart and I spread them wide, and then his body is between my legs, the head of his cock pressing against my cleft.

"Do you want this?" His words are breathy, and I can't believe he has to ask, but I nod.

"Yes."

His whole body seems to relax, as though he's been holding on for that very moment, and he closes his eyes, groaning as he slides inside me, filling me up in a way I've *never* experienced before.

He holds himself there, and I can see such relief on his face, but then he opens his eyes and holds my gaze as he withdraws, and then slowly, slowly slides back in again.

"Fuck you feel amazing." His gaze holds mine, intense and penetrating as he pulls out of me, and then slides back in again. "God, I've wanted you so much!"

He kisses me, and I wrap my legs around his hips. He groans again, his thrusting increasing in speed, the pleasure inside my body spiralling up again until we're both moaning, and I'm grasping at him, my hips thrusting against his as I try desperately to get him deeper.

Soon he grunts, his thrusts slow, and he lowers himself so he's laying next to me, his head resting on my shoulder.

"That was incredible," he says, almost breathless.

He looks up at me, and I reach down to kiss him.

"It was."

"I'm honoured to be your first."

I blush, again, but hold his gaze. "Thank you for making it amazing." I want to be focused on Wulfrun, I really do, but I can't help but wonder what the other four men are like in bed, and whether any of them would have made an equally amazing first.

CHAPTER 15

Wulfrun leans up to kiss me again, but as our lips meet, my stomach rumbles.

"Oops. Forgot I haven't eaten dinner." I laugh, and he does too. I think about a shower I'm feeling so hot and sweaty after that, but now I've realised how hungry I am. I dismiss that thought. I need food, first.

We get dressed and head out past the lounge to the kitchen, where Wulfrun retrieves my food from the fridge and puts it in the oven to reheat it.

Merric appears, his head jerking in a strange manner, until I realise he's sniffing the air like a dog.

He glances at me, and then Wulfrun, his eyes narrowing.

"Right," he says, turning to the fridge to find his meal.

He sits at the end of the kitchen bench, devouring his food cold.

"This tastes like shite, you know Wulfrun." Merric glares at Wulfrun. "All your food tastes like shite."

I frown. Merric is still eating, angrily stabbing his food with his fork and shovelling it into his mouth.

"Can't be that bad if you're still eating it," I say, giving him a pointed look.

He shrugs, turns his glare on me. "Can't starve. Barely surviving here as it is, missing out on having *my* needs filled. Guess we can't all be lucky."

He must've heard us. I feel my face flush and wish I could turn it off, but then I'm just angry. How dare he make me feel like rubbish because I've had sex. It's what I'm there to do, after all. And someone had to be first. It's not my fault there are five of them. I narrow my eyes, but Wulfrun speaks before I can.

"You always this much of an arsehole when you don't get your own way?" Wulfrun's words are angry, but he's smirking, and I can see it's just making Merric worse.

Out of the corner of my eye I see movement in the hall and I glance up to see Ronther disappearing into his room, followed soon after by the gentle click that tells me he's locked his door.

Nice that one of us can escape. I turn my attention back to the standoff in my kitchen. Wulfrun smirks like he's just won the lottery. Merric's shoulders are squared, his hands in fists.

I guess I could escape too, but what will happen if I do? Will Wulfrun and Merric get into a full-on fight? I couldn't bear for that to happen again. I'm so sick of finding them injured by their own acts of violence.

"Just let it go, Merric."

He turns to me. "Let it go? You two reek of sex. If we were out in the jungle I'd be able to smell it a mile away. Talk about rubbing it in a person's face."

I didn't think about that. It never occurred to me that they'd have a super-human sense of smell too, though being part-wolf it makes sense. And since Merric has brought my attention to it, I realise I can smell it too, a mix of body odour and semen and my own juices.

I cringe. "I should've showered. Sorry."

Merric glares at Wulfrun, but seems to answer me. "Nothing to be sorry about. Can't help what you don't know. 'Course, you're the only one here who *doesn't* know how strong our sense of smell is."

Is he suggesting Wulfrun should've asked me to shower? That he deliberately let me come out here smelling of sex?

Merric turns away, but before he does I see the hurt clear in his eyes. If I'd kissed him back earlier, if I'd not pushed him away, he wouldn't be so angry right now. Then again, if it wasn't him, it would be one of the other men.

"Someone had to be first, Merric." Wulfrun is trying to be diplomatic, I can hear it in his tone, but he can't seem to wipe the grin off his face, and it's not helping Merric, who narrows his eyes.

"That someone didn't have to be you."

"Would you have felt better if it was Tormod, or Thyrius, or Ronther?" Wulfrun says Ronther's name as though he's the last person I'd ever have sex with, and I feel a stab of pity for my study companion.

"Would've been better than you." The words are snarled, and for the first time I can see the werewolf side of Merric coming out, even though he hasn't physically changed. Yet.

The thought of them turning werewolf and destroying each other sets my heart pounding.

"Stop!" I shout. "Just stop."

They both look at me.

I hold Merric's gaze. "I'm sorry you weren't the first. I promise I didn't flee the room just to sleep with Wulfrun. I was just... scared. And then Wulfrun was there and—"

"You're scared of me. You're not scared of Wulfrun, but you're scared of me?" He sounds incredulous.

I shake my head. "No. That's not what I meant."

"Sure sounds that way."

"That's because you're not listening! I was scared of the sex, not of you personally, but of giving in to all these... these urges I've been having. Your kiss made me so horny, but I was terrified of what that might mean. I was going to lock myself in my room and have a cold shower, but Wulfrun was there and—"

"And he made use of all those urges."

Merric still sounds angry, but less so, and I'm hopeful I've done enough to calm things down.

"I'm sorry, Merric."

His gaze softens, though when he glances at Wulfrun the anger seems to rise again.

"No more. Not until the rest of us have had our turn."

Wulfrun raises his hands. "She's not an object, Merric. No one else gets to 'have a turn' of her. She says what she wants. If she wants to fuck me again, I'm not going to turn her down."

Merric glances at me, his eyes almost pleading. But before he can speak the door bursts open and Tormod shouts into the house.

"Martha! Wulfrun!" He's striding up the hall, his feet pounding the floor. "Merric! Ronther! Where is everyone?"

I race to the kitchen door, just as he reaches it.

"What is it?" I ask.

"It's Thyrius. He's in the hospital, in a coma."

CHAPTER 16

The hospital is so white. That's my first impression. White walls, white floors, white doors and white ceilings. The doctors wear white, the nurses wear white, the patients' beds are white frames made with white sheets and white blankets and white pillows.

And it's so quiet. The squeak of our shoes on the polished white floor seems deafening, rising above the slight murmur of the doctors huddled together at the desk and the regular beeping of machines.

We're led to Thyrius, in a room at the far end of the corridor, alone except for an older man sitting by his bed.

Thyrius is in wolf form, a bandage wound around his head, and I gasp when I see him. There are all sorts of machines connected to him, making all sorts of beeps and tings and buzzes. There're several hooks above his head, each with a bag and a tube that is somehow connected to his body, one that is definitely blood, another that holds a clearer, silver coloured liquid.

The older man looks up when we come in, his gaze brushing over us until it lands on me.

"You must be Thyrius' wife," he says. "Martha, is that right?"

I nod that it is, and the man glances back to the others. "And his housemates."

I nod again, though the word seems strange to me.

"I'm his father, Dallan."

"I'm Wulfrun." Wulfrun reaches out a hand to shake Dallan's, and introduces the rest of us.

"What happened?" he asks.

Dallan shakes his head. "My father died recently, and a portion of his land was left to my two sons, Thyrius—" Dallan gestured to Thyrius, lying so still on the bed, "—and his brother. They couldn't agree on how best to divide it. It's quite mountainous, with a river that separates the land. Thyrius suggested they just use the river as a natural boundary. It's not an equal split, but it is an easy one. I thought Thyrius was going to take the smaller half, just to make things easy, but next thing I know they're both in wolf form, slashing and tearing at each other." He shakes his head again. "I don't know what set it off, things were going so well, they were discussing it all so amicably."

"Can you ask Thyrius' brother?" I ask.

Dallan's gaze lands on me, and his eyes just look so hollow. "Thyrius' brother is dead. He lost too much blood. And now the doctors are telling me I might lose Thyrius as well."

"Oh." I feel such a stab of empathy for this poor man who has only recently lost a father and now at least one son, possibly two. "I'm so sorry."

Dallan shrugs. "What can you do? This is the way we are. We just have to accept that these things happen." He turns back to Thyrius. "Right now, we just have to hope for the best."

A doctor enters the room and glances over at his patient.

"No change?"

Dallan shakes his head.

The doctor takes a look at the machines and writes something down on a chart, and turns to leave.

"Excuse me," I call, before he disappears out the door. "Can you tell me what's happened."

The doctor glances at Dallan and then back at me. "As you are probably aware, Thyrius was involved in an altercation this afternoon. From that he has suffered a deep gash to the head. Unfortunately we can't be certain of the outcome of this type of trauma. If he survives he may be unable to walk or talk. He may well need constant care for the rest of his life."

I feel the blood drain from my face. Poor Thyrius.

ONE GIRL FIVE HUNGRY BEASTS

When the doctor leaves the room we gather around the bed, and I take the chair opposite his father.

"Hold on, Thyrius," I whisper, stroking the side of his face. "Come back to us."

We don't stay long, but I promise Dallan that I'll be back to sit with Thyrius as soon as I can. The trip home is silent. There doesn't seem to be anything to say.

I'M BACK at Uni the next day, though I can't possibly focus on anything. Dawn asks me about my evening. There's a suggestive tone to her voice that suggests she's really asking if I've slept with any of the men yet. I don't want to talk about it, so I tell her instead that Thyrius was attacked and is in the hospital, and we're all a little bit shocked about it all.

"Oh no! I'm so sorry," she says, the sympathy clear in her eyes.

I shrug my shoulders. "Thanks," I say. "It's just so hard. Why do they have to fight so much?"

Dawn shrugs. "I guess it's just their nature. No one actually holds back, do they? Like with the arena. Once a challenge is laid down, it has to be met. There's no way to get out of it. And they're always encouraged to fight out their problems."

"It helps with population control," another woman sitting at our table speaks up. "Sorry to interrupt," she says, "but I couldn't help but over hear you. The men are encouraged to fight each other, because then if one kills the other that's one less man to worry about. One less man to fight for the few women that exist." She shrugs. "It's harsh."

I nod. "I've heard that. I just wish I could stop it."

The woman grins. "You can," she says. "You can have regular sex with all your men, to keep them happy and lower their frustration levels, and you can give birth to daughters, so that future generations don't have so much to fight about."

"Not like we can guarantee any of that," I say. "Though perhaps we can also teach our sons that violence isn't the answer."

"You can try. Won't do much if the rest of society teaches him different though." The woman smiles and shrugs and I turn back to Dawn.

"How are things going at your house?" Perhaps if I turn the attention back on her I won't have to say anything else, I can just listen.

It works. Dawn spends the rest of the lunch hour filling me in on the comings and goings of her men, none of whom seem to have gotten into any fights, for the time I've known her, at least.

I comment on this and she shrugs.

"They haven't, yet. That doesn't mean they won't. They aren't landed gentry, like your men, though."

"Landed gentry?" I frown. "What do you mean?"

She raises a brow. "You've never thought to find out their history? They're not regular citizens, Martha. Each of your men comes from very wealthy families. Merric is probably the richest, though, Thyrius isn't too far behind."

"What?" I'm gobsmacked.

"It's why they've been involved in so many fights. Because they have land and inheritances to fight over. None of my men have that."

Is that why Kirela selected them all? She seemed annoyed with me for not taking part in the selection process. Was it to spite me? Or does she just want to reduce the male population too, and figured five arrogant, selfish men would be most likely to fight each other if they had to share a woman?

I tell Dawn my thoughts, but she just laughs.

"I don't think it was deliberate. Just the way it went. Kirela knows Wulfrun and Guthram, of course, but that doesn't mean she knows the others. I only know because Wulfrun and Guthram still keep in contact, and Wulfrun told Guthram all about it. You're reading too much into it."

AFTER UNI I head to the hospital to sit with Thyrius for an hour or so. Sometimes his dad stays with me, telling me stories of Thyrius when he was a boy, or of Thyrius' mother, who left them both when Thyrius was a boy to move in with a different group of men. It's proof for the voice in my head that says that there is no guarantee of a happy family, for anyone.

The next few days pass much the same, though I

spend my afternoons locked away in my room, to study alone. Both Ronther and Merric keep looking at me, Ronther with such a longing in his gaze, and Merric with such a hunger, that I find it better to hide away. I'm too worried about Thyrius to even think about having sex right now, though Wulfrun finds a way to touch me at every opportunity, whether it's to brush his hand across my lower back, or simply brush his fingers against mine as he hands me my plate at dinner time. I don't know if Tormod has noticed the tension. He seems lost in his own world, though whenever I'm out of my room he seems to be able to sense it. He appears by my side, following me from room to room until I excuse myself and hide away in my bedroom again.

FINALLY THYRIUS WAKES UP, and within a day or two he is released from the hospital. His speech is a little slow, and his walk is a bit of a stagger, but mentally he's still there. The doctors are hopeful for a full recovery. I feel so relieved to have him back, even with the obvious troubles, and I take the following day off Uni to help him settle in again at home, making sure he has everything he needs.

"Thank you, Martha." He smiles at me as I tuck him in bed for an afternoon rest. "You are very good to me."

I hold his hand until he drifts off to sleep, then

creep out of the room, careful to close the door quietly so I don't wake him.

Merric is waiting in the hall.

"How is he?" he asks, his voice a hush.

"I think he's going to be okay."

"Good." Merric takes my hands. "I know you were worried about him. We all were. But he's home now, and everyone thinks he's going to be okay, so—"

He stops speaking, his gaze burning into mine.

"So?" I shouldn't ask the question, it's so obvious what Merric wants.

He doesn't speak, just puts his hands on my shoulders and pushes me against the wall, his mouth on mine, his tongue down my throat. One hand releases a shoulder and finds its way up the inside of my top to squeeze a breast, but then he groans and pushes himself away.

"I'm sorry. I'm so sorry. I shouldn't be forcing myself on you like this." He turns, but I reach out and touch his arm.

"It's okay, Merric. I want to do this with you." It's been over a week since I've been with Wulfrun, and Merric's advances have just unlocked all that need that I've been repressing since Thyrius' injury. My body is on fire all of a sudden, and all I want is to be with someone.

Merric's eyes widen, his pupils so big I can scarcely see his irises.

He leans down to kiss me again, his tongue

forcing its way between my lips. He's so hungry for me, I can feel his desperation, his need.

He reaches between my legs with one hand, sliding his hand up and under the skirt I'm wearing, pushing aside my underpants until he finds my cleft, his fingers rough between the lips of my vulva.

"You're so wet." His voice is breathy, surprised, and I kiss him again before replying.

"That's because you turn me on."

His eyes widen again, and then he grins, coming close to kiss me again as he inserts first one finger then two inside my vagina.

"Fuck you're hot." He pushes my underpants to one side as he frees his cock from his trousers.

"Here?" I ask looking around.

He shrugs. "Why not. No one's home. It's not like Thyrius is going to jump up and join us."

I'm about to suggest we move, but then his thumb finds my clit and he begins to rub it, and all thought vanishes from my mind.

He grins, and pauses just long enough to pull my top over my head and release my bra so it falls to the floor. He presses me against the wall again, lifting me enough so he can slide me down over his cock.

He groans again, closing his eyes as though to savour every moment.

I wrap my arms around his shoulders, pressing my upper body against his.

"You are keen," he murmers. He takes both my

hands and holds them above my head, and lowers his mouth to cover a nipple and suck, hard.

I gasp. It hurts, but the pain is mingled with pleasure in a way I'd never thought possible and I grind myself against him. He flicks the nipple with his tongue, before sucking, hard, again.

I moan, and grind my hips against him. My clit is tingling, and I'm desperate for it to be touched, too, but he's holding me up, thrusting with such speed my hips are banging against the wall, and I'm gasping as the breath is very nearly knocked out of me. Finally he leans back a little, releasing my arms and rubbing my clit with his thumb.

"Come for me, Martha," he says, his voice husky. "Come on, I want to see you come."

He's so forceful, and I never expected I'd like it like this, but the pleasure is shooting up my spine and my eyes are rolling back in my head as I grind myself against his thumb and his cock, and soon I'm moaning and groaning, too.

"I'm coming, Merric, oh my god, I'm coming! Oh fuck!"

As soon as the words are out of my mouth he's thrusting into me with such force I almost feel like he's going to push me through the wall, but then he comes, giving another couple of hard thrusts before withdrawing and lowering me so my feet are once again on the ground.

We're both panting, and I can feel the combination of his sperm and my juices pooling in my underwear. It's warm and sticky, and I am definitely in need of a shower.

"Fuck, that was amazing." Merric looks at me. "You're amazing."

I laugh. "You're not too bad yourself." I lean up for a kiss. "But I think I'd better go and have a shower."

He glances down and laughs, and I realise he can see the dribble down my leg.

"Might be a good idea. Wouldn't want the other fella's smelling me on you. Might get jealous." He grins, and I see he's teasing.

"Not that anyone living here would get jealous," I tease back.

"Not at all."

In my room I set the shower to hot and turn it on as far as it will go, sending out a blast of water to wash away everything. Merric was so hard, rough even, and yet I feel absolutely incredible after that. I slide a finger between my legs to circle my clit. It feels so nice, and I think back to Merric, pounding me against the wall, as I begin to stroke and rub my clit, faster and faster until I'm coming again, right there in the shower.

I wonder what the others are like. I realise with a start that I want to fuck them all, I want to know all their differences, and all the things that are the same. I want to know what each can give me that I couldn't get from the others. I want to feel five different cocks inside me, and five sets of hands on my body.

ONE GIRL FIVE HUNGRY BEASTS

I turn off the shower and dry myself. Outside I hear the front door close and the murmur of conversation. Someone else is home.

A thrill travels my spine as I wonder who it is, and I marvel at this side of me. It's like something has been unlocked, some need I was never aware I had that's been given a taste, and now needs more to be fully satisfied. I feel like I could fuck all day and not be content.

I've got to find out who just came home.

CHAPTER 17

*L*eaving my room, the house seems quiet. I head up the hall past the lounge to see Merric back on his game. He sees me peering in and glances over, a grin spreading across his face.

"Want to play?" he asks, patting the seat beside him.

I shake my head. "Not right now. Maybe later."

"Cool."

He turns back to his game and I head out through the kitchen and into the garden.

All quiet here.

Back inside I see that Ronther's door is slightly ajar. He must be home.

I knock, and push the door open.

He's at his desk, working at his computer, as usual. He glances up, his eyes lighting up when he sees it's me, and I feel a warm fuzziness spread through my chest. He really is such a sweetie.

"Hey, how was your day?" he asks.

"Good." My mind goes straight to Merric, pounding me against the wall, and I feel myself blush. "Just wondered if you could help me out with something?"

"Sure, anything. You know that." He smiles, his eyes glancing down at my empty hands. "Not study related then?"

"No." I close the door behind me and walk over to him, taking the chair next to him and swivelling it around so it faces him directly.

I hold his gaze, and I see the way his eyes light up the moment he realises what I want, and then cloud over almost instantly from his doubt.

I lean forward, bringing my face close to his. He doesn't move. I'm not even sure if he's breathing. I press my lips against his, but it takes a moment for him to unfreeze. Slowly he raises an arm to rest a hand on my waist. Then his other hand reaches up to cup my cheek, and finally, finally his lips start moving, pressing back against mine.

I pull back, catching his eye again.

"That was nice," I say, watching him as he bites his lower lip.

"It was," he says, nodding.

"Do you want to do more?"

He seems surprised I've asked the question.

"Do you... uh... do *you* want to do more?" He repeats the question back at me.

I run a hand along the top of his thigh, leaning in close to kiss him again.

"Yes," I whisper, and I feel the shiver that travels through his body.

"You need to know, before you start, that I, uh... I've never been with anyone before."

I smile. "That's okay. I've only been with two, and that's been within this last week or so." I grin at the thought, and feel the damp pooling between my legs as I remember Wulfrun's head between my legs, and Merric pounding me in the hallway. Anyone could've walked in and seen us, and we probably woke Thyrius from his nap, but that thought of being caught, of our sex being witnessed, in some way or another, just turns me on more.

"But, what I'm saying, is that I might not be very good." Ronther holds my gaze, and now it's his turn to blush, his face the deepest red I've ever seen on another person.

"And what I'm saying," I say, standing up so I can straddle him, and get as close as I possibly can, "is that I'm only new to this too, and I'm sure we can work things out together."

He seems to relax a little at that suggestion.

I can feel his cock straining against his pants, a thick bulge pressing against my cleft.

"How do we start?" he asks, shifting in his seat.

"Like this." I lower my head so my lips meet his,

and apply a very gentle pressure with my tongue until his lips part, and I can slide my tongue inside.

He tastes like mint. Sweet and bright and refreshing. His hands hold my hips. He seems too scared to do any more, so I take one and place it on my breast.

His eyes widen, his pupils dilating in what I'm sure is a combination of fear and desire, and he squeezes gently, his other hand coming up to take hold of my other breast.

He's so gentle, and his caresses feel so nice.

I pull away, smiling at the slight look of disappointment that crosses his face as I kneel on the floor.

"This is something I haven't tried yet," I say, pulling down the zipper on his pants.

He slides his bottom forward in the chair slightly so I have easier access, his hands gripping the side of the chair as he watches, wide-eyed.

I slide a hand in under his underpants and wrap it around his cock. He gasps, then licks his lips. I gently pull his cock out, and it stands, thicker than the others, I'm sure. The veins around the outside thick and bulging.

Now I lick my lips, and I lean forward to run my tongue across the tip.

He gasps again, and his cock jerks away from my mouth. I wrap a hand around it, marvelling again how smoot and soft the skin is, and yet how hard it feels underneath. This time I hold on as I circle the head of his penis, before opening my mouth as wide as I possibly can to take it all inside my mouth. It's so big, and I quickly realise that taking his entire penis inside my mouth is not something I'm capable of doing right now, but I suck anyway, bobbing up and down on the end. He moans, and I glance up to see his head thrown back. A surge of joy races through my body, that I am able to give such pleasure to someone else, and I'm motivated to see how far I can take it.

"God, Martha." His words are breathy. "That is incredible."

I release his cock and run my tongue up and down his shaft, his panting turning me on, just as well as I can see my sucking is turning him on.

I'm still so wet from Merric, from orgasming in the shower, and now from this, and I desperately want to feel Ronther inside me, so I stop, and stand up.

"Don't stop, please." He's almost begging, and I grin.

"Not stopping," I say, leaning down for a kiss. "Just moving to somewhere a little more comfortable."

I take his hand and pull him over to his bed.

I direct him to lay down on his back, and pull at his trousers, until I have both them and the underpants in a pile on the floor.

His cock is straining, and he begins to pull it, desperate for release. I remove my own clothes, all of them, and climb on the bed to straddle him.

Ronther pulls his own shirt off, and as I lower myself over his shaft, he arches his head up and takes a nipple in his mouth.

"Oh my." I moan in pleasure. He flicks at my nipple with his tongue, then circles, then sucks. He's so very gentle, completely unlike Wulfrun and Merric, and I feel a tingle travelling my spine at his touch. I reach down to play with my clit as I begin to ride him, sliding carefully up and down his cock. He lays back, and I lay on him, my breasts pressing against his chest, and kiss across the top of his shoulder and up his neck.

"Fuck me, Ronther. Please." I don't realise how desperate I am until I hear the words come out of my mouth, but it seems those words are all he needs to finally take some action. He starts to thrust, slowly and gently and first, but in no time he's built up speed. His hands are on my hips again, but this time it's with purpose, to hold me as he grinds his penis deep into my cleft. Soon we're both panting, and as the pleasure spirals up through my head he comes, making several jerky movements before slowing down to a stop.

We lay in silence for a while, catching our breath.

Finally I push myself up on an elbow to look at him.

"Was that good for you?"

"Oh, my, god." He shakes his head. "That was like nothing I've ever experienced before, and so much better than I ever imagined it could be." He glances at me. "What about you? Was it good for you?"

I grin. "It was marvellous for me," I say. "I'm looking forward to doing that again."

"Can we?" he asks. "Right now, I mean?"

There's a knock on his door, and Tormod pokes his head through.

"If you've got a second Ronther, oh. Shit. Sorry. Didn't realise." He starts to close the door, but I call out.

"Wait." He glances at me, an eyebrow raised.

An idea has sparked in my mind. I almost can't believe I'm actually going to do this, but I'm scared I'll lose the opportunity if I don't at least ask. I glance down at Ronther.

"Do you want to try something else?"

Ronther raises an eyebrow.

"Like what?"

"What about a threesome. You, and me, and Tormod?"

Ronther hesitates, glancing from me to Tormod and back again.

Meanwhile Tormod has entered the room properly and is holding the door only slightly ajar behind him.

Ronther shrugs his shoulders. "Sure, why not. Whatever you'd like to try, I'm up for."

I glance at Tormod, who closes the door behind him.

"If you're sure?" Tormod asks.

I nod. "I've never been more certain." The grin on my face widens, and I can feel myself getting wetter by the second.

As he unzips his trousers I see his cock is already bulging. He drops his trousers and underpants to the floor and steps out of them, pulling his t-shirt over his head. I can't help but watch as he takes his cock in his hand and gives it a few strokes. Even when Ronther lifts his head to suck and squeeze my nipples again, my attention is on Tormod, on his incredibly toned body. When he comes up behind me and kisses me on the shoulder, I know for certain that this is going to be amazing.

CHAPTER 18

I'm so sore the next day. Muscles in my legs and torso and face that I never knew existed are aching from the sexual gymnastics I managed the night before. Being with both Ronther and Tormod was amazing, even more so than I expected it to be. I'm so glad I was brave even to ask, and Ronther was brave enough to be open to the idea and give it a try.

But despite these new pains I'm feeling fantastic. I've never felt so content with my life before, so happy with where it's at, so satisfied, about anything! I can't keep the grin off my face, and Dawn knows exactly what I've been up to the moment she lays eyes on me.

"You did it!" She squeals, jumping up and down and wrapping me in a hug. Half the room turns to look, and I find myself laughing and trying to shush her, all at once.

"You did do it," she says, her voice a loud whisper. "I can see. You've never looked so happy in the whole time I've known you."

"I did," I confirm, the grin on my face spreading. "And you were right. It was amazing! And I did enjoy it." I pause a moment, before adding. "I really, really enjoyed it, with at least four of them."

She raises a brow.

"So you didn't enjoy it with one of them? Or you haven't tried him yet? Or are you saying you went four at once?" Her eyes are wide at that, and I laugh.

"No. Not four at once. Two at once was pretty incredible though."

"Three at once is better." Dawn grins, and I can't help but let out a shriek and a giggle at her admission.

Neither of us can concentrate on our classes that day. We sit up the back, giggling and gossiping, earning harsh glares from our lecturers more than once. I never ever thought I'd be one to kiss and tell, but Dawn opens up about everything and I find myself doing the same, comparing our different men, and their methods, and even what we personally liked and didn't like.

"One to go, hey," Dawn comments at the end of our last class.

It's been on my mind all day. But he's still so injured. "I can't do anything about it yet," I say.

"Won't be long." Dawn nudges me with her elbow. "These Werewolves heal up so fast."

"Mostly. But Thyrius is a bit slower than usual, and this was a deep wound."

"Maybe all he needs is a bit of extra special attention?"

THE THOUGHT STICKS with me all the way home. Dawn said it suggestively, like sex would help him heal faster, but I'm so scared of injuring him any more that I wouldn't have sex with him, not yet, anyway.

At home Merric pats the couch next to him, his eyebrows raised suggestively.

I shake my head. "Got to check on Thyrius."

"Don't be too long." He gives me a cheeky grin, and I know what he's thinking.

In the kitchen Wulfrun and Tormod are actually speaking, though the moment I enter the room their attention is broken and both their eyes are on me.

They both move towards me, but Tormod is already closer and he reaches me first, greeting me with a hug and a kiss, and I see a flash of irritation across Wulfrun's eyes. Wulfrun jostles him out of the way, wrapping his arms around me and kissing me.

Then Tormod pushes Wulfrun out of the way to give me a gift.

"Woah, guys. It's okay. I'm not moving out, I'll be here all day, I'll come back here again after Uni tomorrow, and the next day, and the day after that. I literally don't have anywhere else to go. You can give me some breathing space."

They both look sheepish, but Tormod still has his hand out, holding out another small box, so I sigh and reach out to take it.

Inside is a pair of earrings, each with a tiny red love sparkly heart.

"No animals?" I ask, glancing up at him.

He shrugs. "I think I've given you enough animals. Besides, Thyrius' presents were beginning to outshine mine, and I can't have that."

I shake my head. "There's no need for competition—"

"A bit of healthy competition never hurt anyone."

I disagree but keep that thought to myself.

"They're beautiful," I say instead, giving him a kiss on the cheek. "Thank you."

"So," Wulfrun interrupts. "What is your favourite food? I realised this morning that I've never actually asked you, I've just been cooking all my favourite dishes. I should cook things you like."

"Well, my mother used to cook a delicious apple pie—" I barely get the words out before Tormod is dismissing them.

"Who needs food when you have alcohol?" He picks up a bottle of wine from the bench and holds it out to me. "Can I pour you a drink?"

I shake my head. "Thanks, but no. I was actually heading in to see how Thyrius is feeling." I glance at

Wulfrun. "Has he had much to eat and drink today? Perhaps I could take something in?"

Wulfrun takes a jug out from a cupboard. "It's been a while since he's had his water refilled. You could take some fresh water in."

He fills up the jug and hands it to me, his fingers brushing mine as I take it from him.

I thank him and leave the room, wondering exactly when these men will actually grow up and acknowledge that this situation is not the best for any of us, but fighting over me isn't going to help at all.

When I enter Thyrius' room, he's propped up in bed, his head thrown back, gently snoring.

I try not to wake him, but the process of putting down a full water jug and picking up the empty one seems to make enough noise to cause him to stir. He opens his eyes, lifting his head to look at me.

"You're home." His speech is still slow, but I can hear that he's improved a hundred fold from the previous day.

I shake my head. "You werewolves really do heal quickly, don't you?"

He smiles. "It takes an awful lot to keep a wolf down. Don't you worry about that."

I pour him a glass a water and hand it over. He winces a little as he readjusts himself on the bed, waving away my arm reaching out to help, and then takes the glass.

"You do quite a good job looking after us all, with all our fights and injuries."

I laugh. "It's not like I have a choice."

"You do. You could focus on your University studies and ignore us. It's not like we are anything much to you, other than men forced into your life."

I reach out to take Thyrius' hand. "You started out that way, but things have changed since then. You've all become special to me."

Thyrius smiles and pats my hand with his spare one.

"I'm glad to hear that."

He closes his eyes and lets his head drop back onto the pillow.

"You are still tired, aren't you?" I ask, but it's so obvious I don't wait for an answer. "I'll let you rest. I'll come back again later and see how you are doing."

He nods, his eyes still closed.

"Do you want me to help you lay down?"

"No." He shakes his head, the movement barely there. "This is comfortable enough."

I lean over to give him a kiss on the forehead and slip out of the room.

It sounds like Tormod and Wulfrun are still in the kitchen, once again talking civilly to each other, so I decide to go and check on Ronther.

He's absorbed in his computer, sound-proofing headphones on. He won't know I'm here unless I go over and touch him, but he's so intent in his work I don't want to disturb him, so I just close the door quietly behind me and watch him for a while. He really is the sweetest of the lot and the easiest to get along with. Aside from the fight in the arena, which wasn't something he could back down from, he seems to avoid fights and conflict, and sex with him the other day was nice.

A message pops up on his screen, and even from this angle I can see the frown at his interrupted work, so I back quietly out of the room, and join Merric, who is more than happy to see me for another of his computer games.

"Feels like ages since you've sat here with me," he comments.

"Only a few days, surely."

He frowns, and rubs his chin. "I think it's longer. Must've been trying to avoid my animal magnetism."

I laugh and give him a friendly punch on the shoulder.

"Of course. I just didn't want to throw myself at you and end up fucking right here on the couch. That's absolutely it."

He grins as he passes me the device.

"Absolutely."

CHAPTER 19

The week goes by quickly. At home there's still a mostly friendly rivalry going on, but overall everyone seems happier and less frustrated. At Uni I'm enjoying my new intermediate classes. Soon, we're told, we'll be able to make decisions on what type of career we might like to work in, in this society. We're given a huge list of options and told they're just a sample of career opportunities present here in the city. It's so broad I wouldn't even know where to start, though Dawn is certain she just wants to stay home with the many children she plans to have. I don't see why we can't have children and a career, especially with five husbands to help out with the childcare.

At home, Thyrius improves in leaps and bounds. After a week or so he's back to sitting up in bed and strumming his guitar, and it doesn't take too much longer for him to start singing along. It's a sure sign he's on the road to recovery, and I spend an hour or so each afternoon with him, sitting by his bed to begin with, then moving out into the garden as he gets stronger.

He's quite sweet, and it's nice he's no longer competing with Tormod to buy me the best gifts. In fact, he seems nicer now he's *not* competing. The bump to the head certainly did one thing, it made him realise what is most important in life.

Soon his speech and movement are back to normal, and I'm hopeful that he feels ready to take our relationship to the next level.

The only way to be sure is to ask.

I've avoided having sex with the other men, even though they've asked. It's stupid, really, because I'm so horny, and clearly they are too, but I feel like I should be fair with them all, and make sure I have some time with everyone once, before I fuck any of them again.

Unlike the others, Thyrius doesn't seem at all wound up, and part of me wonders if he's not interested. Perhaps he decided to leave once the twelve months is up? I'm so nervous about approaching him that when I do finally decide to ask, my heart begins to race, and my hands are so sweaty.

He's working from home today, hiding away in his room attempting to get some paperwork done. I've given him an hour. I can't hold on any longer, and surely he needs a break by now, too?

I'm holding a tray with a jug of water and two glasses on it, and carefully balance it first in one hand and then the other, as I wipe my hands on my pants, take a deep breath, and tap gently on his door.

"Yes?"

I open the door and peer in.

"Just me," I say. "Just wondering if you'd like a drink?"

"You must've read my mind." He smiles, and I enter the room, closing the door behind me. I set the tray on his desk and pour out some water each.

"What are you working on?"

"I've just had to finalise the paperwork for the palace I'm building on my new land."

"Your new land? You mean, the land you won in a fight with your brother?"

He frowns. "It wasn't my choice to fight. I didn't want him to die."

I bite my lip. "Sorry. That wasn't very thoughtful of me. I shouldn't have said anything."

He waves away my apology. "It's fine. It's true, what you said. And yes, that land. I want to build something beautiful, a place we can live, once you've finished your University studies."

"We? Me?"

He nods.

"And what about the others?" I ask.

He shrugs. "It's going to be enormous. There'll be room for them too, if you want them there."

I nod. I can't really think about any of that right

now. "Actually, I'm here to ask you about something else, too."

Butterflies are dancing in my stomach, and I swallow. Thyrius looks at me.

"Yes?"

"I was wondering, if, maybe, you'd like to meet me tomorrow. At the University."

"At the University?"

I nod again. "There's a really beautiful spot on the grounds, a stand of trees, with a creek running through it. I was thinking of skipping class, so we know no one else will be there…" I trail off, I can't bring myself to ask the actual question, but I don't think I need to. Thyrius' eyes are wide, and there's a grin across his face.

"You want to take things further?" he asks, wrapping his arms around my hips and pulling me closer.

"Mm-hm." He tilts his head up, and I bring mine down to press my lips against his.

"I'm looking forward to it."

I'm so nervous the next day that I can't possibly focus on any of my classes, or Dawn, or anything anyone says to me.

By midmorning Dawn is frowning, and she taps the side of my forehead with her finger.

"Hello! Is anyone in there?"

I shake my head and force myself to meet her gaze.

"I am, I'm here. Sorry." I realise she's been speaking about her husbands, and I really should have been listening.

She peers at me.

"Are you all right?"

I shake my head. "I'm really not feeling well, to be honest." It's not entirely false, my stomach is churning, and my heart is racing. "I think I might find somewhere to lay down for a while. Or maybe go home." Her question is quite good timing, really, because this next class is the one I was going to miss, to catch up with Thyrius.

Dawn is nodding. "That sounds like a better idea. Go home, rest. It's about time those men had their turn caring for you, after all the time and effort you've put into caring for them."

I nod and excuse myself from the room.

Outside I need a drink of water to try and calm my rising nerves.

I leave through the main door and follow the path that would lead me home, but at the last minute I turn and follow another path, down through a copse of trees, past all the university buildings to a small stream.

Here there's a low bridge, and the path meanders alongside the stream for a few hundred metres until it comes to a clearing.

I'm early, but Thyrius is already here.

"You made it."

"Of course." He grins. "Wasn't sure how much

time we had, thought I'd better be early so we could make the most of it."

I grin and he takes two strides across the clearing and wraps me in his arms, his lips pressing hungrily against mine.

I didn't realise how desperate I was for his touch, how much I needed it, longed for it, until his hands were on my breasts, squeezing and kneading. I tear at the buttons on his trousers.

His hand finds its way into my pants, and he circles my clit, gently rubbing, not the clit itself but all around the edges.

"You're wet already," he says, his voice almost breathless.

"I've been imagining this all day," I whisper back. "In fact, I've been dreaming of this moment for weeks."

He pulls up my top to suck at my nipples, and I moan as he slides a finger between my lower lips and pushes it deep into my cleft.

I grab at his shoulders and moan.

He pushes my pants down, then undoes the zip on his own trousers to pull out his cock. It's the biggest I've seen, certainly the largest of all my men, and I gasp. I'm glad now, that Thyrius was my last. I think if he'd been my first I probably would've ended up a lot sorer afterwards.

He hears my gasp, and he sees me looking at him. A wolfish grin spreads across his face.

"You ready to be impaled?"

I meet his eyes and I find myself breathless. I nod a yes.

He lays me on the grass and begins to rub the head of his cock against my clit.

"Do you like dirty talk?" he asks.

"I don't know," I admit.

"Shall we try?"

I nod again, suddenly mute.

"You're about to be fucked by a werewolf," he says, his voice a low growl. "You ever had werewolf cock before? Thick fat cock pounding you, filling you up?"

His words send a delicious shiver down my spine, and I'm not sure whether it's the morning's daydreaming, or the words, but combined with his cock pressed against my clit I'm losing control already, my orgasm spiralling up, and I let out a loud, long moan of pleasure.

He chuckles. "You do like that."

He slides inside me, and I wrap my legs around his waist.

"You like being in public? You like the possibility someone might stumble across us at any moment, fucking right here in the woods?"

I can't speak, my whole body is tingling, and I reach down to find my clit and rub it, as he begins to pound, faster and harder.

"That's it, Martha. I can see you like it. Never thought you'd like werewolf cock, I bet. Won't be able to get enough of it now."

He's pounding me so hard now, I'm being jolted against the grass, but I'm barely aware of any of it as the pleasure explodes through the top of my brain, and I'm moaning again as the orgasm rips through me.

Soon he's coming too, and he collapses on me, spent.

"That was hot." He grins down at me. "Especially you playing with yourself. Fuck that was hot."

"Glad it turns you on," I say.

Suddenly there's laughter from further up the path, and we both scurry to get our clothes on.

"Sounds like we're not the only two planning to make use of this spot," Thyrius says with a laugh. "I'd better get home. And you'd better get back to your classes." He leans in for a quick kiss before disappearing through the trees, leaving me to follow the path back past the couple heading my way.

My face is burning, it must be so red, but when I pass the guy and girl heading towards the clearing I nod a hello.

They whisper something to each other, and burst out into giggles. I feel some sort of strange happiness. I have five partners, and I've slept with them all. Two of them at the same time.

Hot.

I think about going back to my classes for the rest of the afternoon, but if I do Dawn will wonder how I had such a sudden improvement, and I'm really not sure I could concentrate anyway. Instead I take a slow walk home, sneaking into my bedroom for a shower before any of the men see me. That quickie with Thyrius has me horny for more, and I masturbate in the shower, and then come again in bed. I'm so tired and I feel so satisfied and content that I end up falling asleep.

CHAPTER 20

My dreams are filled with sex. I don't always see the face of the person I'm with, though everyone's face comes in and out of focus at one point or another, Merric, Wulfrun, Thyrius, Tormod, Ronther. They're all there, all giving me pleasure.

A knock on my door wakes me, and for a moment I'm a little disorientated. Where am I again?

"Are you home, Martha?" Wulfrun calls through the door.

I push myself up in bed.

"I am. Just a minute."

I climb out of bed, scrambling for my dressing gown as I realise at the last minute that I didn't dress after my shower.

I unlock the door and let Wulfrun in.

"Are you okay? We heard you missed some classes today."

I raise an eyebrow. "And where did you hear that from?"

"I was just out to do some shopping, and I came across Guthram. Dawn was with him. She asked if you were feeling better."

Ah. So the city is smaller than it looks after all.

"You didn't skip classes today, did you?" Wulfrun raises a brow.

"Maybe."

He looks shocked.

"Don't worry, it's only going to be a one off. And it was for a good reason." I lift my chin, and I can't help but smile at the memory of my quickie with Thyrius.

Wulfrun nods. "You are an adult and capable of making your own decisions," he says. "It's good to see you happy."

He gives my shoulder a squeeze and heads down the hall.

"By the way, dinner will be ready shortly."

I nod my thanks, though by now he's already in the kitchen. I close the door so I can get dressed.

Merric isn't in the lounge, in his usual spot, and as I wander through the house, I discover Ronther isn't working in his room, either. There is a large amount of chatter coming from the back of the house though. I walk through the kitchen, filled with the smells of something delicious in the oven, and out into the garden.

They're all here. Ronther reclining with a beer, Merric helping Wulfrun pick some salad greens for dinner, and Thyrius and Tormod in conversation.

"Woah." I say as I take in the scene. "Do I know you people? You all look familiar, but none of you seem to be acting the way I've come to expect."

They all turn to grin at me.

"We're all feeling pretty happy with things at the moment," Ronther says, lifting his beer to me in a 'cheers' movement.

"So I see. This is unusual."

"Well, we have a partner, even if she is one we have to share," Merric says.

Thyrius speaks up. "Yes. And she, or should I say you," Thyrius gives me a pointed look, "seem to be really relaxing into this strange relationship we're forced into, and at the moment, speaking for myself here, but I dare say everyone would agree, the future looks quite promising."

"I'm glad to hear it."

Ronther holds out a beer to me, and I accept, twisting off the cap and taking a seat next to him.

I lean back and just listen to the conversation swirling around me. I can't believe it. For the first time all my men seem to be actually getting along.

Dinner is soon ready, and Tormod sets the outdoor table while Wulfrun dishes up, and Thyrius brings out some drinks.

ONE GIRL FIVE HUNGRY BEASTS

The meal is eaten with jovial banter, and I can't help but shake my head as Merric and Thyrius actually agree on something for once.

"What's the shaking head for?" Tormod notices, and asks me.

"I can't believe how well you guys are getting along. It's great. I like it."

"It could have something to do with the fact we've all been laid." Merric smirks at me, and I feel my face flush.

"That cheers you up, does it?"

"Well, masturbating only lets off a certain amount of steam," Merric continues. "Actually having actual intercourse with an actual woman is pretty fantastic, really. And now you've done us all once, I'm assuming we all get another turn pretty soon?"

There's a hopeful note to his voice, but I'm still stuck on the idea that they all know.

"So, you've talked to each other about it?"

"You could say that," Wulfrun says with a grin, and Tormod interrupts.

"Talked isn't quite the word you're looking for there. More like, boasted. Wulfrun was the first of course, and then Merric. We might never have known you'd gone for Ronther if it wasn't for Tormod raving about how he caught you in the act and you asked him to join the two of you, and how hot that experience was. And, of course, Thyrius was injured, so we all knew it would take some time before anything happened between the two of you."

"Tormod said you seemed to enjoy having sex with both of them at the same time. Is that something you want to repeat?" Wulfrun asks, but before I can respond, Thyrius speaks.

"Unless of course you preferred one of us, or some of us, over the others? In which case maybe we *won't* all get another turn."

"So what Thyrius is asking," Tormod interjects, "is who did you like best?"

I'm speechless for a moment. They're all so different, and I like those differences, but I suspect if I say as much they'll just think I'm trying to be diplomatic.

"Well, Merric was kinda forceful—"

"He didn't hurt you did he?" Thryius interrupts before I have a chance to finish, and Merric glares at him.

"I didn't literally force her, Thyrius."

"Hey." I put my hands up in the air, hoping for their attention. "Merric didn't force me. He's just forceful. There is a difference. I don't like being forced. But I did like the way Merric didn't hold back."

Ronther glances down at his drink. "Can't have enjoyed it with me, then. I wasn't like that at all."

Ronther is sitting across the table from me, so I reach out and cover his hand with mine. "I loved it with you. It was nice to be able to lead, and that you listened to exactly what I wanted and what worked for me. Honestly."

He glances up, and I see he's hesitant to believe me, but I hold his gaze, and he nods.

I continue. "And then when Tormod joined us, that was amazing, and I'm so grateful you were able to open to that, without being jealous or possessive."

Ronther's face flushes a little, but he nods and squeezes my hand. "Thank you. I wasn't sure about the threesome myself. But I really enjoyed it too. It was quite hot, really, watching you, seeing how much the situation turned you on."

"I'm glad."

Wulfrun turns to me.

"So, you really did enjoy the threesome?"

I feel my face flush, but I nod. "I did."

"And you'd do it again?"

I nod again. "I would."

"What about with more than two men?"

I hesitate for a moment. More than two men? What on earth would I do with more? But then the thought sends my libido racing, and I know I'd have to try it at least once.

"How many more?"

Wulfrun eyes off the other men before returning his gaze to me.

"How about all of us?"

There's a murmuring around the room, and I can see a mixture of excitement from Thyrius, Merric and Tormod, and uncertainty from Ronther.

"Would you all want that?" The question is more to buy me time than out of any need to ask it.

"I'm keen," Merric says.

"I'd give anything a go, at least once," Thyrius says, a grin spreading across his face.

"If it's anything like a threesome, I'm in." Tormod seems to have a matching grin.

I glace at Wulfrun. "You suggested it, so I'm guessing you'd be up for it."

Wulfrun nods. "There's a bit of jealousy still amongst this group, even though we're doing well to control it. Perhaps group sex on the odd occasion might be a way to keep that in check, providing everyone is in agreement, of course."

I nod, and turn, finally, to Ronther.

"You don't look so sure."

He shrugs. "The threesome was hot, I've already told you that. But five of us? How could you possibly take five of us, all at once?"

I lift my shoulders. "I don't know. That's my question, too. Wouldn't some of you be missing out, some of the time? But I guess unless we try it, we'll never know." I hold his gaze. "Would you like to try it?"

He's quiet for a moment, but I see his pupils dilate, and I know before he nods his head that he's in.

I NEVER IMAGINED there would need to be so much preparation for an orgy. Wulfrun is insistent that it will probably take time, and we should have food and water on hand so we can snack if we get hungry.

ONE GIRL FIVE HUNGRY BEASTS

Tormod wants to treat it like a party and drags out the last of the alcohol from the party he threw me earlier. Ronther is mostly avoiding everyone, though I sense that's more from being unsure what to do, rather than anything else.

After much discussion it's decided that everyone's bedrooms and beds are too small for five people, and Merric has cleared away his video game equipment from the lounge room so that he and Thyrius can drag out two of the mattresses and place them side by side on the loungeroom floor. We have extra blankets if we need them, and the couch and armchair if someone wants to try something different.

Tormod grabs some massage oil from the bathroom, and Ronther finally comes up with something he'd like to do to contribute, and lights numerous candles all around the room.

Finally everyone is happy that we have everything we could possibly need.

The room looks gorgeous. The candles give a lovely warm glow to the room, and there are so many soft comfy spots to recline in. It looks so cosy and safe, and I realise that any fear or uncertainty I may have had about this situation is gone. It's been replaced by excitement instead.

"So," Ronther starts the conversation. "How do we start this?"

All of a sudden there are arms around my waist, and a kiss on the back of my neck. I shudder, but it feels so nice, and I close my eyes as Wulfrun continues his kisses along my collar bone, and then up my neck to my ear.

I feel someone in front of me and open my eyes to see Merric. He grabs a breast through my top, massaging it as he lowers his lips to mine. I arch my neck so I can kiss him better and he puts his other hand on my other breast.

Wulfrun nibbles on my ear, but his hand moves down to brush my leg, ever so softly, as he pulls up my skirt.

I feel more kisses on my other shoulder, and Thyrius whispers in my ear.

"You like this? You like the attention of five men? Is it making you wet? Is it making you horny?"

A shiver travels my spine, and I moan my reply. If I wasn't kissing Merric I'd say yes. This *is* making me horny. I can feel Tormod and Ronther's eyes on me, on us, and that is turning me on, too.

Merric lifts up my top, breaking the kiss, and disturbing the others, to pull it up over my head. He throws it on the floor and drops to his knees, taking my right breast in his mouth. Tormod jumps in at that opportunity, grabbing and squeezing a breast as he kisses me.

Wulfrun's hand, at least I think it's Wulfrun's hand, slips into my underpants, a finger circling my clit briefly before pushing up inside my vagina. I moan again, and that seems to spur them on, now I have a man on either breast, one sucking on either ear and a hand stroking my insides.

I'm so absorbed in all the sensations, every part of my body being touched, but part of me is aware that they aren't all taking part. Someone is still sitting out.

Ronther.

I open my eyes, and beckon him to come closer. The other men must have noticed because they shuffle aside, and Ronther stands, reaching out to take my hand, and steps into the circle of men, like a wall around me. I lick my lips as I pull him closer, and he leans down so his lips meet mine.

We kiss, and I reach up to hold his head close. There is so much happening to my body, I just want to return the favour somehow, and I push my tongue between his lips to find his, flicking at it and opening my mouth wide, almost as though I could devour him.

Someone unzips my skirt and slides it down my legs, following soon after with my panties. There's kisses on the outside of my leg, and soon a head between my legs, more kisses trailing up my thigh as I do my best to widen my stance without tripping over someone.

There's hot breath on my cleft, then a tongue, quickly dabbed against my clit and taken away again. It returns, held there for the briefest of moments, before a series of short sharp dabs send waves of shudders up through my spine, and I'm gasping into Ronther's mouth.

I swear, I can feel the mouth between my legs

grinning. There's a tongue again, slipping from one end of my vulva and back again, and now my legs give way, someone behind me catching me.

They lay me down, and I see each man is miraculously trouser-less, stroking their cocks as they touch my body. Merric moves between my legs, now he is licking and sucking on my clit, one finger then two delving inside me, sending me into the throes of ecstasy.

Thyrius comes up close to my head, his cock waving in the air close to my mouth. I open up, arching my neck to get as close as I can.

"You want to suck me off?" He's speaking in that gravelly voice again, and it's sending me wild. He brushes the tip of his cock against my lips, and pulls it away.

"Please."

"Please?"

"Please, let me suck you?"

Merric sucks on my clit again, and my whole body arches in response.

"God, Thyrius. Just bring it closer."

He raises an eyebrow, a smirk on his face, as he rests his cock on my lips.

"You like sucking cock, eh? Thick werewolf cock, deep in your mouth."

He's not deep in my mouth, not yet anyway, and yet now I'm desperate to see how far I can push it.

I open wide, bobbing up and down on the head, and reach up to grab his hip and pull him closer. I open my throat wider. I still can't take him all, but I get a good part of him in my mouth, and I can see out of the corner of my eye when he throws his head back, his groan of pleasure vibrating down through his body.

"Fuck, that's good."

The comment spurs Merric, who is leaning over me now, and I feel the head of his cock press against my vagina.

I bob faster, closing my eyes and letting a groan escape around Thyrius' cock as Merric presses his into me.

There are still hands on my breasts, but someone else has taken one of my hands and wrapped it around their cock, and I begin to pull on that as I bob on Thyrius and Merric thrusts into me.

"Gonna share?" Tormod is behind Merric, and Merric glances up at him with a grin.

"Sure."

Before I'm fully aware of what's happening Merric has rolled us both over, and now I'm on my knees, straddling him.

Someone is thoughtful enough to usher Ronther over, and I reach out to take his cock, running my tongue up and down the length of it before opening my mouth to cover the head.

He groans, running his fingers through my hair.

"Fuck that feels good, Martha."

I moan. It's the only way I have to express my

pleasure, but then there's someone behind me, and a tongue is circling my anus.

My eyes open in shock and surprise, not that there is anything I can do about it at the moment. It only takes a second for the shock to pass, and this new pleasure to register. I close my eyes. It feels amazing. Soon the tongue is probing my arsehole, and a hand has reached around and is stroking my clit, while someone else sucks on a breast.

It's almost too much to bear, so many sensations coming at me all at once. But then the tongue on my arse stops.

"You want to try anal?"

I freeze for a moment, and Ronther pulls away as Merric also comes to stop.

I turn back to look at Wulfrun. "Anal?"

"I'm told it's nice, if we're gentle, and you relax."

The thought had never occurred to me before, and though my initial reaction is to be a little squeamish of the whole idea, my body seems to be desperate for more of any sort of touch.

I nod. "As long as you're gentle."

Wulfrun nods in return, and leans up to kiss me ever so softly on the lips. "You say stop, and I'll stop. Instantly. No questions asked."

I take a deep breath, and face forward again to find Tormod in front of me. I open up for his cock, bobbing up and down a couple of times until I feel Wulfrun's cock press against my anus. I take a deep breath and do my best to relax.

ONE GIRL FIVE HUNGRY BEASTS

He feels so big.

I return my attention to Tormod, imagining my whole body opening up, welcoming them all, and letting the pleasure flow through me and fill me up.

Wulfrun pushes a little deeper, and I wince.

He must've sensed it because he stops, but I reach out a hand to stop him from withdrawing.

"Keep going," I say. "It feels incredible. Just, gently."

He has some sort of lubricant he squirts onto his cock, and he tries again, the liquid cold on my skin. This time it's easier, and he gently rocks his hips back and forward, thrusting a little deeper each time.

I give Tormod's cock a little tug, and he brings it closer again, and as I close my mouth around him, I reach out to take Ronther's cock in one hand, and Thyrius' in the other.

Soon Wulfrun is completely inside me, and Merric is as far as he can go without causing me pain. I've never felt so full in all of my life. I'm stroking the cocks of Thyrius and Ronther, but I can't control much else as Merric and Wulfrun thrust into me at my lower end, and Tormod thrusts gently into my mouth.

I'm lost, as pleasure spirals up and bursts through the top of my head, and I'm moaning around Tormod's cock, and my body is arching and writhing all on its own.

Suddenly Ronther comes, his sperm spraying out over my hand and arm. It seems to be the catalyst that sends them all off, moaning and groaning, Merric and Wulfrun grinding into me before they too release their seed inside me. Thyrius covers my other arm, and Tormod sprays into my mouth, and I swallow and suck until it stops flowing, licking and cleaning his cock before I let it fall from my mouth.

"Fuck."

Merric's arms have dropped to his sides, his head is lolling back off the edge of the mattress.

There's laughter, and groans of relief, as everyone finds a spot to fall into. I collapse onto Merric. There's no way I can move any further at the moment, and he manages to lift one arm to wrap it around my shoulders.

"That was incredible," Wulfrun says, leaning over me to give me another kiss on the shoulder, before slumping to the side.

"I'll say," Thyrius responds with a sigh from his spot lounging on the couch.

"I certainly enjoyed it," Ronther admits, a lazy smile on his face.

"We're not done are we?" Tormod asks.

Everyone laughs, though I'm not entirely sure that Tormod is joking.

"You fellas seem to be spent," I say.

"So you could go again?" Tormod's brow is raised. I tilt my head to one side.

"What? You're not done?"

"I haven't had a turn at penetrating you yet."

"You're a bit too limp to manage that at the moment, Tormod." Wulfrun is teasing, but instead of getting upset, Tormod grins.

"You just give me a moment, and you'll see what I can manage." He begins stroking his cock again, and I can see it won't be long before he'll be ready for more. For some reason the thought seems to wake me up, too.

I roll over, and begin to rub my clit. "You come and lick me out, and I'll fuck you again."

The grin on Tormod's face widens, and he's between my legs faster than I thought possible.

"You smell like sex," he says with a grin. "I like it."

He reaches out with his tongue to stroke from perineum all the way to my clit, and I throw my head back, and spread my legs wider.

"Fuck that's good." I glance up at Ronther and Thyrius. "I want you both inside me, too. After Tormod's spent again, of course." I grin at Tormod, and he grins back.

"I'll be longer this time, baby. Don't you worry about that."

I FEEL REVITALISED after sex with Tormod, and I'm still hungry for more after Thyrius fucks me, too. Ronther is still hesitant, even after seeing how enthusiastic the other men were, and I find myself having to coax him. But there's something sweet about that, and caring, and when he has also come inside me I snuggle down with him on the mattress, my head resting on his chest, and his arm around my shoulders. The other men are scattered around, either asleep or very close to it. I can hear soft little snores, and Merric, who has scarcely moved, opens one eye blearily as I lay down, and rolls over to snuggle up closer behind me.

For some reason my memory flashes back to my first day in the city, being led through that large building with Kirela, and confronted by all those men.

"What would any woman do with five husbands?" I'd asked. Did she know the answer? I would've been horrified if she'd suggested we have an orgy. How could any woman cope with more than one man at a time?

How naïve I was. A smile creeps across my face as I snuggle down amongst my men. Clearly, there is plenty that can be done with five husbands, and I'm looking forward to doing it again, and again, and again.

FOR YOU: A SPECIAL OFFER

Thank You For Shopping At The Romance Queen!

Get a *special* discount on your next purchase by visiting:

www.romancequeenbooks.com/specialoffers

COPYRIGHT

© Copyright 2019 by Hollie Hutchins - All rights reserved.

In no way is it legal to reproduce, duplicate, or transmit any part of this document in either electronic means or in printed format. Recording of this publication is strictly prohibited and any storage of this document is not allowed unless with written permission from the publisher. All rights reserved.

Respective authors own all copyrights not held by the publisher.